Animus Est Vista

Drue Fairlie

Published by Drue Fairlie, 2023.

ANIMUS EST VISTA

First edition. June 15, 2023.

ISBN: 979-8201960742

Written by Drue Fairlie.

Also by Drue Fairlie

The Ghosts of Summer
One Percent
The Catspaw Incident
Animus Est Vista
Requiem of Shadows
The Trouble with Hitchhiking
The Anchored Heart
Midnight and Grey

Table of Contents

Animus Est Vita

By

Drue Fairlie

Chapter One

"Wow," said Will as he stepped out of his car and looked up at the forbidding building in front of him, "this looks like a friendly place."

"Can I help you?" asked a light, pleasant voice.

Will took his eyes from the old Edwardian edifice in front of him and looked at the owner of the voice. He had dreaded this job ever since he had received the call from his agency on Friday night. It wasn't that he disliked care homes, but Crabtree Lodge was on the very outskirts of the town and Will considered anything outside the town centre as being in the country, and he hated the country. But now as he looked at the pretty, slim, young brunette who had addressed him he felt that perhaps this would not be that bad a job after all.

"Can I help you?" said the brunette again, only this time a little more sternly.

"I'm Will McCormick," said Will holding out his hand, "the agency sent me, I'm meant to start work here today."

"You mean you were meant to start here two hours ago," corrected the brunette.

"Yes, sorry about that but this is a hell of a place to find."

"Yes, well you're here now," said the brunette curtly, as she turned towards the lodge, "my name's Marie Mallory and if you'll follow me, I'll show you to the manager's office."

Will cast his eyes skyward in a 'not another jobsworth' appeal to the heavens, fell in behind Marie and followed her into the lodge.

As Will walked in through the large double doors of the building, he noticed a faded Latin motto carved into the arch above them.

"Animus Est Vita," he said slowly mouthing the unfamiliar words.

"It means the soul is life," said Marie when she heard him utter the words under his breath.

"That's cheery, this must have been a really fun place back in the day."

Will's guide to the manager's office stopped in her tracks, turned to look at him and said, "Seeing as this place was built as a hospital for children with consumption, and as the Edwardians had no cure for that rather nasty little disease, I doubt that very much."

"What a charmer," Will muttered to himself as Marie walked off.

The inside of Crabtree Lodge was no less gloomy than the outside. Will stepped through the large, ornate entrance into a well-lit communal hall that had three long, wide and rather drab looking corridors running off it, two to the right and one to the left. In the middle of the initial corridor was a large, old-fashioned photograph of an Edwardian man in his mid-fifties with a bushy moustache, surrounded by a group of about a dozen children. The man had a benevolent, kindly expression on his face and the children looked up at him lovingly. One of the figures, a small boy of about ten years old caught Will's eye because this was the only one of the children not looking up at the man. Instead, this young boy must have been staring at the photographer when the picture was taken, because it seemed as if he was staring out of the picture, something that Will found a little unnerving.

"This way Mr McCormick," Marie said, pulling Will's attention from the photograph and directing him to the first door on his left. "Mrs Cutter can see you now."

"Thanks, Marie, it's been a pleasure," said Will sarcastically.

"Yes," said Marie with a cold smile, the sarcasm in her voice equal to Will's own. "I'm sure it was."

Before Will could try and reply, Marie had walked off and a voice from inside the manager's office said, "Come in, Mr McCormick,"

Will watched Marie walk off a moment longer then stepped quickly through the door.

"My name's Molly Cutter, Mr McCormick," said a middle-aged woman, seated behind a large, oak desk on the far side of the office, "please take a seat."

Will walked quickly across the small, rather cluttered room and sat down across from the lodge manager in the only other chair.

"Look," he said," I'm sorry I'm late. I know it's not a good way to start but I simply couldn't find this place."

"Please Mr McCormick," said the manager smiling, "or may I call you Will?"

Will nodded in answer, rather taken aback by the friendliness of the manager after his curt reception from Marie.

"Please Will, think nothing of it. I'm sure it was a one-off, and you're right; this place can be quite difficult to find if you've never been here before."

"That's very considerate of you Mrs Cutter,"

"Please it's Molly," said the manager with a smile, "now, about what we would like from you. Did the agency explain what we are looking for?"

"Not really, only that you wanted some kind of night staff."

"Yes, kind of, but it is a little more complicated than that. What we're looking for is a kind of a jack of all trades. Someone who can turn their hand to almost any kind of job that needs doing overnight and can work with little or no supervision."

"You do know that I'm not a nurse, don't you?"

"Oh yes of course. There is always nursing staff on no matter what the time. What we need is someone who can do all those little jobs that need attending to."

"That sounds like something I can do. I like to be busy; it makes the shift go so much faster."

"That's just what I like to hear. Now, there is one more thing I would like to tell you, and that's about the staff here."

Will leaned forward and said, a little apprehensively, "Yes?"

"They all like a joke now and then, and sometimes it can get a little out of hand, and as you're going to be the new boy, shall we say that you are going to be their prime target."

Will felt himself relax somewhat when he heard this. He'd worked for agencies for most of his professional life so the concept of being the new boy and the butt of jokes was something that he had long ago learned to take in his stride.

"Don't worry about it, Molly," he said confidently, "I'm used to that kind of thing."

"That's good to hear, Will, but just so you know what to expect let me fill you in."

Will didn't reply he just sat back and waited for the manager to continue.

"The older members of staff here have a rather peculiar welcome for new starters."

"Let me guess," said Will with a smile, "superglue in the locker catch? Or maybe cling film over the toilet at night? What about being sent for a glass hammer or a rubber nail? But after seeing this place I would have to put my money on that old favourite, the ghost story."

The manager stared open-mouthed at Will for a moment, then burst into a genuine, if short-lived giggle.

"How did you know?" she said, impressed by his guess.

"As I said, I've been in this line of work for quite some time. But I would like to know what to expect."

"I think the best thing would be for me to take you to the staff room. From there Marie can give you a full tour of the place, tell you your duties and fill you in on what you can expect on your first night."

"Marie," said Will, his smile slipping at the mention of the young woman who had first greeted him.

"Yes," said Molly, noticing his reaction to the name. "She's the assistant head nurse here. Why, is anything wrong?"

"No, nothing at all," said Will quickly, "shall we go?"

The pair of them walked out of Molly's office and into the main corridor. As they walked, Will said, "This is a huge place."

"Yes, it is. We have twenty-eight rooms here at Crabtree Lodge, plus several out-buildings and something over five acres of grounds. All in all, the entire place is quite a size."

The pair of them walked on down the corridor making small talk until they came to the last door on the right. As Molly opened it she said, "Here we are, the staff room. If we've timed it right someone should be making a cup of tea."

Will was ushered into a room the like of which he had seen throughout his working life. On the far wall opposite the door was a row of battered-looking lockers with people's names scrawled on them, next to a faded poster from Turkey. A rickety-looking table in one corner had what looked like the world's oldest electric kettle on it and half a dozen mugs, none of which were the same, sitting beneath a handwritten rhyming sign asking people to wash their cups when finished with them. Next to the table was a small, off-white fridge that had seen far better days and hummed louder than it should. For the staff to sit on there were four straight-backed chairs, one with wheels, two very old and overstuffed armchairs, a bench, and strangest of all a deck chair.

Will smiled as he looked around the room, and thought to himself, "This is like coming home."

"Ah," said Molly, as she walked into the room, "looks like we missed out this time, but tell you what, let's get the kettle on. The day shift should be here any moment now for their tea break. And there's nothing like having a cup of tea ready for everybody to make a good first impression."

Just as the two of them started to prepare for the day shift's mid-morning tea break, Will wondered what form his initiation would take.

"I bet it ends up being some silly sod in a bedsheet," he thought, a half-smile crossing his face as he searched the brown Formica cupboards for tea bags and coffee.

"Here they come now," Molly said, nodding to the door as it opened and ushered in a hand full of men and women, all of them talking at once.

"Hello everyone," Molly said, her voice rising above the good-natured conversations, "I'd like to introduce our newest member of staff, Will McCormick."

"Hello," said Will, half-heartedly as every head in the room turned and looked at him.

There was a moment's silence, and then an older, plump woman in a dark blue uniform said, "Well I hope he's got the kettle on or there's going to be trouble."

This broke the ice that had grown over Molly's announcement and suddenly everyone was talking at once and introducing themselves as Will handed out cups of steaming hot tea to eager hands.

While he was doing this Molly came over to him and said, "ah, here's Marie. If you would excuse me, Will, I'll go and talk to her and see if we can't get your tour underway and get you a start time for tonight."

Will watched his new boss walk over to Marie and thought, "a tour with the ice queen that should be interesting."

Will's attention was drawn away from the two women by a voice at his side saying, "so you're the new night guy then? Well, I hope you last longer than Jim."

Will turned to find that the owner of the questioning voice was a short, balding man heading towards his fifties.

"Sorry, what did you say?"

"I said," started the man again, but before he could continue the woman in the dark blue uniform interrupted him.

"Enough of that, John. Let the poor boy start his job before you get going on him."

The balding man looked at the woman for a moment, then wandered off mumbling to himself

"Don't let John bother you," said the nurse, smiling and holding out her hand, "he likes to try and wind up the newcomers, but sometimes he can be a bit of a bore about it. My name's Sally I'm the head nurse here."

"Will," said Will taking the offered hand, "and it's ok, Molly's already warned me about this place."

"Oh," said Sally, a surprised look on her face, "and you're still taking the job?"

Before Will could ask Sally what she meant Molly appeared beside him and said, "Are you ready to go, Will?"

"Yes," said Will putting down his untouched tea, "whenever you are."

"If you go with Marie, she'll show you where everything is and what you have to do tonight."

Will turned to look at Marie, who mouthed the words, "after you," as she held the staff room door open for him.

As she watched the young, blonde man walk out of the door Sally turned to her boss and said, "he said you told him all about this place Molly, is that right?"

"No of course not. I told him that the staff here has this ghost story initiation thing they do."

Sally didn't say anything in reply she just looked at Molly reproachfully.

"Don't look at me like that Sal, what could I do? I couldn't tell him the truth, could I? We've had three people for that job in the last three months. Word's getting around about it, I was lucky to find him. His was the last agency in town that would send me anyone."

Chapter Two

On the tour of his new workplace, Will discovered two things. One that Crabtree Lodge was just as massive as it had looked on the outside, and two, that Marie Mallory wasn't the ice queen she had at first appeared to be. The first thing that Marie had done once she and Will had left the staff room apologised for her abrupt behaviour when he had first arrived.

"I didn't mean to be such a bitch this morning," Marie had said as they walked down the corridor that led back to Molly's office, "it's just been so mad here of late, what with more patients and the staff shortages I feel like I'm always here and never at home."

"I bet your husband loves that?" Will said, speaking before he thought.

He instantly regretted what he had said when he saw the look that passed quickly over Marie's face.

"I'm sorry, I didn't mean anything,"

"It's OK Will," she said, holding up her left hand to show off its ring less appearance. Its only adornment was a faded circle of pale skin on her third finger, "there was a husband, but that's finished now. And life's the better for it."

"Look, Marie."

"Just forget it, Will, you didn't mean anything I know that, and we all say things we regret. I did this morning, you did now. Let's call it even shall we?"

"Ok," Will said, somewhat relieved that he hadn't destroyed their fledgling friendship, "so where do we go now?"

"The morgue," she answered, not missing a beat.

"What?"

Marie looked at him for a moment and then burst into a fit of laughter.

"It's ok," she said, taking his arm in hers, "it's not a morgue anymore. We just call it that to get a reaction from the newbies. It's where we keep the clinical waste bins."

"That's OK then, so it wasn't a morgue?"

"Oh yes, it was."

Their route to the out-building that had once served as the hospital's morgue took the pair of them down a side corridor and through a large dusty room that had once been used as a school for the children who had been treated at the hospital. The old schoolroom was the first place in the huge nursing home that seemed in any way to have a light air about it. It was only being in this room that made Will realise that the rest of the building had such an oppressive feeling about it.

"I like this place," he said as the pair of them walked through the large, windowed room, "it feels kind of welcoming."

"A lot of people do, some of the older staff say this is the one place they feel safe here."

"Safe?" said Will looking at his guide, "what do you mean safe?"

"You know, relaxed, comfortable," said Marie a little too quickly, "they use this place as a kind of impromptu staff room, somewhere to come for a little piece of quiet."

"Oh ok. For a moment I thought that this was going to be the start of my initiation."

"Initiation?"

"It's OK, Molly told me all about it, how you all like to get the new boy going with ghost stories and the like. Well, I just thought that you were going to start it off. You know this is the one room where people feel safe from the spirits of the old, spooky lodge."

"No, nothing like that," said Marie, as she opened the door at the other end of the now disused classroom, "I don't get involved in that kind of childishness, I had enough of it when I was a trainee nurse to last me a lifetime."

The rest of the tour took the pair the best part of an hour. Kate showed him the out-buildings, including the old morgue, and the vast grounds. Then she took him to meet a few of the more nervous patients. The ones that liked to know who the new members of staff were and when they were starting.

The last room they came to belonged to Crabtree Lodge's oldest resident. Just before she opened the door, Marie said, "this is Joan Reedums, she's a lovely old lady but she can be a little strange sometimes."

"Strange?" Will asked.

"She talks to people who aren't there and says that she sees a little boy at the end of her bed."

"You sure you're not trying to get me going?"

"She's a patient Will and that's something I don't joke about. It's not her fault she has these episodes."

"Sorry I didn't mean to joke."

"No, it's OK; everyone says I take my job a little too seriously. Maybe they're right. Anyway, let's go meet Joan."

As Marie opened the door Will heard the old woman inside the room talking.

"Yes, I know. Alright, you'd better go they're here now."

"Hello, Joan," Marie said, as she and Will walked into the room.

"Hello, dear," Joan said smiling at the young woman happily, "Hello, Will."

Will stared at the old woman opened mouthed and said, "how do you know my name?"

"Oh I hear things dear," Joan said, as she eased herself slowly out of her chair, "I hear things. Now, who would like a cup of tea?"

Will and Marie spent the next half an hour in Joan's room. Will found the grey-haired old lady to be both charming and funny, and someone who loved life and lived it to the fullest extent that her frail body allowed. Joan made the pair of them a cup of tea and offered them biscuits that she claimed she had made herself. When Will looked at Marie to confirm this, the young woman simply nodded and smiled as she took one of the offered biscuits. Will took one as well, but he did not know what to expect as he put the biscuit in his mouth. What he didn't expect was one of the most delicious tastes that he had ever experienced.

"Are you surprised, Will?" Joan asked a twinkle in her eye.

"A little, yes,"

"Don't ask me how she makes them," Marie said as she took another biscuit, "we've all been trying to get the recipe out of her for years, but she won't give it up."

"Maybe I'll leave it to you in my will, Marie," Joan said, as she sat down slowly on her bed, "but for the moment if you don't mind, I think I need to rest."

"Oh, Joan," Marie said as she got up and helped the older woman to lie down, "I didn't mean to keep you so long."

"That's OK dear, I like company and if I'm tired then I must still be alive."

"OK then, Joan," Marie said as she led Will to the door, "I'll try and pop back tomorrow if you like?"

"Yes, I'd like that dear, nice to have met you, Will."

"You too, Joan," Will said with a smile, taking a genuine liking to the old woman, "and if it's alright with you I wouldn't mind coming back to see you as well."

"After more biscuits are we young man?"

"How did you guess?"

Both Will and Marie laughed as they left Joan's room. Once the door was shut, Will said, "She's nice."

Marie didn't answer but she did hold a finger to her lips and tilted her head to indicate that Will should listen. As they stood there in the hallway outside Joan's room, they heard the old woman talking.

"Yes, I know, well what else could I do? I had to be nice. Please don't be like that. You know I still love you."

As Joan continued her one-sided conversation Marie signalled for Will to follow her back down the corridor. Once they were out of earshot of Joan's room Will said, "What was all that about?"

"Joan suffers from bouts of senility," Marie said sadly, "but for a lot of the time, she can be incredibly lucid and aware. We all love her to bits here. I think everyone has a soft spot for her and her biscuits, which by the way she buys from the local shop here, but we never let on that we know. She can have very bad bouts where she doesn't know who she is or what's going on. When that happens, she may seem like she's talking to people who aren't there. And that can get a little creepy."

"But how did you know she was going to start talking to herself when we left her room?"

"Because she always does that, at first, we thought she was doing it on purpose, you know, to maybe freak the staff out. But now we think that someone visiting her acts as a trigger and starts her having an episode."

"OK, but why show me?"

"Because like I said I hate the whole initiation thing that goes on here, and I especially dislike it when some of the staff use people like Joan in their games. Believe me, sooner or later someone is going to bring you up here at night and tell you the story about mad old Joan and the ghosts she talks to."

"But how did she know my name? That was weird."

"Not really, I've seen that one before as well. I bet you next month's wages that someone was up here as soon as we left the staff room telling Joan your name just on the off chance that I'd bring you here."

"That's bad."

"Yes, it is and as soon as I find out who it was, they're fired. But for the moment there's not much I can do about it apart from what I've just done. But if you do hear who's responsible I would be very interested to know."

"And I'd be glad to tell you," Will said. He felt no loyalty to anyone who tried to use people like Joan.

"That's the end of your tour," Marie said as they walked out of the main entrance, "your shift starts tomorrow evening at ten and now that you know where we are I imagine you won't be late."

"No," Will said, holding his hand out to Marie for a second time that day, "I'll be here on time."

Marie looked at the young man's offered hand for a moment, then put her hand in his. Shaking it gently she said, "goodbye Will, see you tomorrow."

As she watched Will walk out to his car Molly walked up behind her and said, "Did you take him to see Joan?"

"Yes," said Marie simply, as she turned to look at her boss, "but do you think this is all necessary?"

"Yes, I'm afraid I do, we have an inspection coming up in a few weeks and if we don't have a full complement of staff then we might just lose our licence. And I don't want to take the chance of losing any more night staff to stupid childish ghost stories."

"Are you so sure they're stupid Mol?"

"Yes, I am," Molly said, looking at the young woman sternly, "and so are you, OK?"

"OK, Molly, whatever you say," Marie said as she turned and walked back into Crabtree Lodge, "whatever you say."

Chapter Three

Will felt a real sense of excitement about his new job as he drove back to his midtown flat. It seemed like money for old rope to him. All he had to do was keep his head down, do what he was told, and he could keep this job for ages. Or at least for the six months, he needed to save up the rest of the money he needed for his trip to Australia.

"Six months," he said to himself as he drove, "six months, and its sand, sea, and who knows what else."

As he pulled up at a set of traffic lights, Will felt his phone vibrate and a voice in his earpiece said, "Hi, Will, how did it go?"

"Hi, Max," Will said, smiling as he heard his sister's voice. "Yes, it went well, I start tomorrow."

"What's the place like?"

"It's like something out a fifty's horror film. Let me go home, grab a shower and I'll come round and tell you all about it OK?"

"OK BB, see you soon."

Once his phone went dead Will turned up his radio and sang along to it all the way home.

Two hours later Will pulled up outside his sister's beautiful, detached house. As he got out of the car, Jason, his sister's four-year-old son, and his ever-present basset hound puppy, Bob, ran up to him shouting, "Uncle Will!"

"Hi J," Will said, catching his nephew as he jumped into Will's arms and spinning him around. "How are you doing, big man?"

"Again!" Jason said in answer as Will tried to put the boy down.

Will knew from experience that there was no way he could get into his sister's house without at least another two spins for Jason and a furious belly rub for Bob. By the time the three of them made it to the front door, Jason was dizzy, and Bob was barking loudly and tripping over his oversized ears. Will's sister Max was standing there waiting for her brother with a smile on her youthful face. It always amazed Will that his older sister looked so much younger than he did.

"Hi sis," he said as he gave Jason his last spin, "what's for dinner?"

"And what makes you think you're invited to dinner?"

"It's takeaway," Jason said, as he breezed by his mother still spinning, "and you can sit next to me, Uncle Will."

"Mmmm," Will said as he kissed his sister gently on the cheek, "takeaway."

"Yes, takeaway," Max said as she kissed her brother in return, "but you can only stay if you tell me all about this new job."

"That sounds like a deal."

The takeaway turned out to be a curry brought home by Max's husband Brian.

"Hello, Will," Brian said as he came into the kitchen holding two bags brimming with food containers.

"Hi Bri, how's the job going?"

"Cosmic," Brian said, as he put the bags down on the kitchen table and loosened his tie. "I almost stayed awake for the whole day today."

"Daddy!" shouted Jason as he saw his father standing in the kitchen.

"Hi J," Brian said as he scooped his son up into his giant arms and hugged him tightly.

Seeing this always gave Will a warm feeling deep inside. Because Brian Howard could not look less like a doting father and loving husband if he had tried. Brian was a giant of a man well over six feet tall and close to two hundred and fifty pounds. This combined with his shaven head and arms coved in tattoos gave him the appearance of a bouncer in some seedy back-alley night club, rather than the accountant that he was.

"What's the job then, Will?" Brian said as he put Jason down and started to sort through the bags of food.

"Word gets around quickly, doesn't it?" Will said looking at his sister.

"What could I do?" she said in answer to her brother's question as she passed her husband some plates. "He's bigger than me."

When Will looked back at Brian the big man was doing his best scowling face to show Will just how scary he was.

"Stop that, Bri," Will said, "it looks like you need the toilet."

Jason and his mother burst out laughing, and then they both scowled at each other.

"What a bunch of muppets," Will said as he tried in vain not to laugh too.

"So, what is it?" Brian asked again as his laughter died to a chuckle, and he started to pile food onto plates.

"It's working the night shift at Crabtree Lodge."

"Crabtree Lodge?" Brian said, his face full of surprise, "I didn't realise you were that brave."

"Go on then, Bri," Will said as he put his plate down, "tell me all about it."

"Not while J is awake, maybe later."

Will looked over at his sister for an explanation to her husband's sudden change in mood. But all Max did was look back at him and shrug her shoulders.

Will loved being with his sister and her family, they always made him feel welcome and at home. It was a place for him to come when the world was just a little too cold and unfriendly. Both Max and Brian had tried to talk Will out of making his trip to Australia, but he had told them it wasn't going to be forever; just six months and then he would be home. And even if he did by some outside chance stay on for longer or even permanently, then they would have somewhere hot to go for a holiday and he would have somewhere cold to come for Christmas.

After they had finished their meal and Will had helped Brian load the dishwasher the three of them went and sat in the small conservatory set at the back of the house.

"Well, Brian," Will said, as he sat down in one of the comfortable armchairs that peppered the small, cosy room, "are you going to tell me about Crabtree Lodge?"

Before Brian could answer Jason raced into the room and threw himself on to Will's lap saying, "Can you take me to bed Uncle Will?"

Brian and Max smiled as their young son's knees and elbows found every soft and delicate area on Will's body.

"If you, ouch, want me, ouch, too, J," Will said wincing as he picked his nephew up and placed him on the floor.

"And I want a story."

"Pardon me?" Max said looking sternly at her son.

"Sorry, mum, can I have a story please?"

"Yes, you can," Max said smiling, "but only a short one, OK?"

"OK."

"Right then, big man," Will said, as he took Jason's hand, "what's the story to be tonight?"

"Can you make one up, Uncle Will, and can you put Bob in it please?"

Will looked down at Bob, who was as ever was just behind the young boy and said, "I guess so, J."

"Great. Come on Bob, bedtime."

Bob barked in answer and ran happily after his young master, tripping over his ears every third step.

Once Jason and Will had left the room Max said, "Are you trying to wind him up about this Crabtree place, Brian?"

"No, not at all," answered her husband as he poured her a glass of red wine. "I'll tell you all about it once Will gets back."

"He's going to be at least half an hour, you know what J's like with his stories."

"Well, if we've got half an hour," said Brian, suggestively raising an eyebrow slowly.

"We can't Bri, not with Will in the house."

Brian just stood there, looking at his wife and smiling, while Max tried to give him a scolding look, but failed miserably.

"Alright," she said, standing up and taking his hand, "but we've got to be quick and quiet."

Just over half an hour later Will came back downstairs after telling Jason a tale of space monsters and heroes with laser guns and talking giant cats, which the boy enjoyed immensely but fell asleep halfway through. Will knew that he would have to finish the story next time he put his nephew to bed. When he walked back into the conservatory Brian handed him a glass of wine.

"So, what's the deal with Crabtree Lodge, Bri?"

Brian poured himself and Max another glass of wine before he spoke.

"You two didn't grow up around here, did you?"

"You know we didn't," Max said, surprised at the tone in her husband's voice. He sounded afraid, something she had never heard before.

"I did, and from as far back as I can remember Crabtree Lodge has had a bad reputation."

"What are you going to tell me, Brian?" Will said sipping at his wine and laughing. "That the place is haunted and I should beware the moon."

"No, nothing like that, but that place is wrong somehow Will. I know that sounds stupid, but it is."

"What do you mean wrong?" Max said, moving closer to Brian as she felt goose bumps break out over her skin.

"Just that, the place is wrong. I've heard some weird things about Crabtree Lodge."

"Like what?" Will said, enjoying the atmosphere his brother-in-law was weaving around the three of them.

"My dad used to tell me about how some friends of his went there one night on a dare. He couldn't go because he'd caught chicken pox, but he told me what happened. His friends told him that when they got there the place was all locked up. You've got to remember that this was long before the place was used as a rest home. My dad's friends tried all the doors, but they were all locked, everyone. But just as they were about to leave, the front door of the place creaked open and they could see a light on inside."

"Oh," Max said softly.

"Yes, oh."

"What did they do?" Will asked, caught up in the story as much as his sister.

"What else could they do? They were young teenagers more concerned about being ridiculed for being afraid than what might have unlocked that door. They went inside. My dad told me that they were in there for less than ten minutes. But his friends said that it felt like hours. None of them could remember what happened. One of them said he could hear voices, children's voices, calling out to him, asking him for help. Another said that he saw a woman dressed in a long flowing dress walking down the hallway reading a book. But the one that freaked me out was my dad's friend Tony. He told my dad that he'd seen old Otto Crabtree himself standing in a doorway at the end of a hallway, smiling at him and beckoning him to go over. Tony said that he was halfway down the corridor before he realised what was happening. It was only the fact that one of his friends lost it and ran out of the building screaming that brought Tony to his senses. The moment he heard that scream Tony took off with the rest of them. And here's the thing, he said that just before he ran out of the front door, he heard Otto screaming his name."

"Shit, Bri," Will said once his brother-in-law had finished his story, "thanks for the nightmares."

"You asked, remember?" Brian said as he got up to refill their glasses.

As Max took her glass from Brian she said, "did you ever go there?"

"Just once, me and a few friends went there one night when I was sixteen."

"What happened?" Will asked, sensing that there was more.

"We did what my dad's friends did, we tried to get in. You see, me and all my friends had heard my dad tell that story repeatedly and it got to be a bit of a bore, so we decided to see for ourselves. We got there just around midnight as they did, and we tried to get in just like them. We checked all the doors and windows, but they were all locked. We even talked about breaking into the place, but we didn't have to because just as we were standing there deciding what to do a light came on inside and the front door started to open."

"Oh my god Brian," Max said, "What did you do?"

"What do you think we did, we took off at just about the speed of light, that's what we did? I tell you that place is wrong. You wouldn't get me in there at night for love nor money."

"You will get me in there for the money," Will said, laughing to try and lighten the mood. "The agency is paying me double for this job, and that will be more than enough for yours truly to get to Oz."

"You're still going then?" Max asked, unable to hide the sadness that crept into her voice.

"Come on Max, don't do this again, it's not going to be forever. It's just something I have to do."

"I know, I'm just going to miss you is all."

"I'll be back before you know it, stealing your food and drinking your beer. But for now, I've got to go."

Max walked her brother to the door and as he left she said, "I'm sorry if I'm being a pain about this Australia trip Will. But it's just so far away."

"I'll be fine sis honest, and anyway I'm sure you'll have lots of things to do while I'm away."

"What do you mean?"

"It's just that when I took J to bed everything was fine," Will said, smiling as he touched his sister's jumper, "and now this is inside out. Makes you wonder what went on while I was storytelling doesn't it?"

Will laughed as he watched Max's cheeks flush a vibrant shade of red. He was still laughing as he got into his car and started his journey home.

Chapter Four

Will spent the rest of his evening doing all the boring jobs that someone who lives on their own hates but must do. He ironed clothes, cleaned the kitchen, and then he 'man vacuumed', meaning that he only vacuumed those bits of floor that he could see, working on the assumption that if he couldn't see them, they weren't dirty.

Eventually, he stopped, poured himself a large glass of Irish whisky, and sat down in front of the TV to look for whatever bad film he could find. Will loved poorly made B movies, the poorer the better. He planned to stay up as long as possible so that he could sleep late the next day and be as ready as he could for his first night shift at Crabtree Lodge.

At first glance, as he flicked through the TV channels, he couldn't find a single thing that caught his attention, but just as he was about to give up he found what he was looking for; an old nineteen fifties black and white horror film called The Night of the Demon.

"Outstanding," Will said, grinning as he read the synopsis.

He had just over forty minutes before the film started, so he made himself a sandwich and poured another generous whisky before settling down to wait.

Will enjoyed the film immensely. The acting was bad, and the special effects were worse, but somehow the overall effect was incredibly eerie and suspenseful and Will found himself quite captured by the menace that the film portrayed. But about half an hour from the end his day caught up with him and Will's eyes started to flutter, and despite his best efforts they closed, and sleep stole him away. He was woken moments later by a loud bang from his bedroom.

"What was that?" he said to the empty room, as he got up and went to see what had happened. When he walked into his hallway, he saw that his front door was swinging open and a large black cat was sitting in the doorway washing itself slowly. As he went to move towards the door to close it the cat saw him and let out a loud high-pitched hiss that had the hairs on the back of his neck standing up in a heartbeat. The cat turned and vanished into the night that waited outside the front door.

"What on earth?"

As the door lock clicked home Will had the disturbing sensation that someone was standing directly behind him, and no matter how hard he tried he could not bring himself to let go of the front door and turn around.

"Who's there?" he called out, still unable to turn around.

His only answer was the sudden soft breath of his intruder brushing against the nape of his neck. It took Will all his courage to turn round and confront his intruder, but when he looked, he was alone in his hallway. His sigh of relief was cut short when he saw the door to his bedroom slowly swing in on itself and the grinning figure of Otto Crabtree, looking just as he'd done in his painting stepped into the hallway.

"Hello Will," whispered Otto from the other end of the hallway.

"You, you can't be here."

"But I am, and I've come for you."

Otto screamed and rushed down the hallway, arms outstretched and hands flexing in their anticipation of grabbing hold of Will.

Will threw his hands up in terror and woke from his nightmare with a shriek; his body covered in a cold sweat and spilt whisky.

"I hate you, Brian," he said, cursing his brother-in-law and his stories as he jumped up and tried to brush himself down. Will's heart was still racing as he went to get a cloth from the kitchen to mop up the spilt alcohol. Try as he might, he couldn't resist looking at the front door just to make sure there was no black cat, and even though the cat wasn't there he went and checked to make sure the door was locked. He let out a small sigh of relief when he turned around and there was no mad, smiling Otto Crabtree waiting with open arms for him, but he still checked inside the bedroom, turning on every light as he went.

Once he had cleaned up, he went and had a shower. The moment he closed the door to his small, cramped bathroom he imagined that Otto Crabtree was standing outside waiting for him. No amount of self-recrimination would shake that very scary notion from his mind. He showered with the bathroom door open and the shower cubicle door ajar and by the time he was finished the floor was awash with water which Will had to soak up with towels. As he stood up with the last water-soaked towel in his hand he caught sight of his reflection in the mirror.

"You're a girl, you know that don't you?"

The mirror Will just stared back at him almost as if he was ashamed to answer.

Once everything was cleared away and he had searched his small flat one last time he went to bed. But as soon as the light went out images of his nightmare came rushing back to hover behind his eyes.

"Ok, I give up."

With that Will got up and put on his coffee percolator. It was going to be a long, long night.

While he waited for his coffee Will went into the sitting room, turned on his TV and started to channel surf. Almost the first thing he came across was a horror film about a young woman caught in her house alone by a knife-wielding maniac.

"No, I don't think so," he said to himself, as he watched the young, fit woman run from room to room of her house. With each door that she opened the film's music swelled. Will knew that it was building to a horrific crescendo but changed the channel long before that happened.

Once the coffee was ready Will poured a good measure of whiskey into it for comfort and then spent what remained of the night watching cartoons. It wasn't until the first rays of the new day's sun glinted through his sitting-room curtains that Will dropped off to sleep.

He was woken from his slumber by the urgent ringing of his phone.

"Hello," he said groggily into the receiver.

"Will?" said Max, surprise in her voice. "Are you still in bed?"

"No," answered her brother, as he stumbled from his armchair. "No, I'm up."

"You sound terrible; I hope you didn't have any nightmares after Brian's story last night."

At the mention of his brother-in-law's story, Will's mind flew back to the previous night and his incredibly real nightmare.

"No of course not Max, I'm not ten you know."

What his sister said next made Will's blood run cold in his veins.

"Lucky you, because I had a right one."

"What happened?"

"I dreamed that old Otto himself was lurking in my hallway. And the scary thing was that he knew my name and when he ran at me, I woke up screaming. I tell you, Will, I thought I was going to have to peel Brian off the bedroom ceiling. My scream even woke little J up. The poor soul was in tears."

Will paused for a moment composing himself before he replied. His sister's dream was almost a mirror of his own.

"That doesn't sound much like fun Max, but it was only a story. You shouldn't take them so seriously."

"Everyone can't be as tough as you. Anyway, I was only calling to wish you luck tonight. I hope you enjoy your first shift at the ghostly old lodge."

"Yes, very good Max, you're not going to freak me out. It's just a nursing home and nothing more."

"If you say so, BB. Anyway, have a good time and tell me all about it tomorrow, OK?"

"OK Max, talk to you tomorrow."

Once he had hung up the phone Will went into the kitchen and made himself a coffee. While he was waiting for the kettle to boil, he thought about what his sister had told him about her dream.

"That's just too weird," he said to the empty kitchen as he lifted the kettle and poured boiling water into a cup.

After a quick bite to eat Will left for his first shift at Crabtree Lodge. It took him longer than he expected to fight his way through the nighttime traffic, but he made it to the nursing home a good twenty minutes before his shift started.

"At least I'm not late again," he said to himself.

Just as he was about to walk across the car park a small, very old mini pulled up alongside his car. Will watched with fascination as the mini created its very own smoke screen just before the engine was turned off. He tried not to smile when he saw Marie get out of the self-camouflaging car.

"Nice car," he said to her as she walked over to him.

"Thanks, but I'm afraid it's not for sale."

"That's disappointing."

"I'm sure disappointment is something you're more than used to, Will."

"Do you have many friends, Marie?"

"A few, but I usually manage to scare them away given time."

Will looked at Marie for a moment unsure if she was serious or not. Then he noticed the laughter that shone in her eyes and said, "OK, you win."

"That's what I like, a man who knows his place."

As they walked through the main doors Will once more looked at the photo of Otto Crabtree that hung there. Even though the photograph was the same as it had been on his interview day there seemed something different about it. Will couldn't quite put his finger on it, but the photo seemed changed somehow, not in content but attitude. What had looked to be a beautiful photograph of a benevolent and kindly benefactor pictured with the grateful children he had helped now appeared to be one of half-hidden malevolence. Otto Crabtree seemed to have lost his gentle smile to have it replaced by that of a predator, and the children seemed to look at Otto with fear on their young faces.

"Looks different at night, doesn't it?" said Marie when she saw Will studying the photo.

"Yes, it does."

"Well don't worry; it's just a trick of the light. I'm always telling Molly to move it. Now let's go and get a coffee and I'll take you through your shift."

Chapter Five

Will enjoyed his first shift at Crabtree Lodge, and in the weeks that followed he found that he was starting to love his new job. His colleagues, who he had initially thought of as stand-offish and rude, turned out to be a varied and entertaining group of people that Will soon became fast friends with. The patients were an amazing mix of people who despite their ailments met life with energy and courage. Even the weakest of them would summon the strength to speak to him as he cleaned their room or emptied their rubbish bins. It was almost as if they saw something in Will that made them want to speak to him and be a part of his life, even if that part was only for the briefest moment. The ghost story initiation that he had been warned about never reared its head and very soon he stopped thinking about it.

Will and Marie started to spend a lot of time together at work and he found himself missing her when they worked different shifts. Slowly he realised that he wanted more from her than just a simple working relationship.

The only thing that Will disliked about his job was the photograph that hung in the main hall. He found something disquieting about it, not that he would have ever told anyone this. His sister and brother-in-law would have laughed, and he just didn't know Marie well enough to voice such childish fears, but whenever he was alone at night he always walked past the photograph as quickly as possible and as far away from it as the corridor would allow. Even during the day when it seemed to lose its power to frighten him Will still gave it a wide birth.

It was after his third week at Crabtree Lodge that Will started to notice something strange about the photograph, or to be more precise, the children in it. He was almost convinced that the small forlorn figures that inhabited the old bronze frame changed places, one with another.

The first time Will noticed this he put it down to tiredness and his eyes playing tricks on him. It had been about two a.m. on the Monday of his third week, and he was walking towards the staff room for a tea break. He had walked past the photograph when something different caught his eye. He stopped and went back and looked closely at the picture. Everything seemed the same, the large smiling man in the centre surrounded by children and the one young boy sitting on the left staring out of the picture. It took him a few moments to realise what was different, and then a chill ran down his spine.

"Weren't you sitting on the other side?" he said to the young boy and felt a childish sense of relief when the boy didn't reply.

"Talking to yourself Will?" said a voice close to him.

Will was sure that his heart stopped for a moment as Marie's breath touched his ear.

"Bloody hell, Marie," Will said as he spun round to look at her, "why don't you scare somebody."

Marie's already large grin grew wider as she said, "Come on you big girl, I'll make you a cup of tea."

As the pair of them walked off a large moth flickered across the hall light, its wings casting shadows across the face of the picture. As the moth's shadows danced and jumped, they gave the illusion that the young boy turned his head and watched the young couple walk away.

The staff room was already filling up as Will and Marie got there for their first tea break. Unlike most places that Will had worked for the staff at Crabtree Lodge all took their tea and lunch breaks together. At first, he thought that this was a little strange but after a few weeks, he found that he enjoyed the company. There was just something about the lodge that made you want to seek out other people and not be alone for too long.

"Are you in the chair, Sally?" Will said as he took a steaming cup of coffee from the large head nurse.

"As always, I always seem to get here first. I'm sure you all hide somewhere till I've got the kettle on."

"So, you're still with us then?" said a curt voice next to Will.

Will turned to see John Anderson, who he had met on his first day and had so far been unable to like.

"Yes, still here, John," Will said trying his best to keep the annoyance out of his voice.

"I'm sure Otto will change your mind sooner or later, or maybe one of the children that run around this place."

"Give it up John. I know there are no ghosts, and you know there are no ghosts, so nice try but I'm getting a little bored with all the 'let's scare the new guy' stuff now."

"You think it's all a joke do you, sonny?" John said, his bald head going slightly red as he became angry.

"Yes, John I do, and I tell you what else. I think someone your age should know a bit better than to keep going on about such fairy tales."

The surrounding conversations in the staff room had stopped when John raised his voice, and now the only thing louder than the silence was the tension that had grown between the two men.

"Alright that's enough," Sally said as she stepped in between the two men. "Just shake hands and cool down. We don't need anything getting out of hand over nothing, do we?"

Will took a deep breath and said, "Yes, you're right, Sally. Come on, John, what do you say?"

John looked at the offered hand for a moment, a moment that reached a little longer than Sally would have liked. Then just as she thought John would refuse it, he reached out his hand and took hold of Will's grudgingly

"Yes, I guess so," he said as he shook Will's hand slowly.

"Good," Sally said with a small sigh of relief as she watched the tension in the room subsided, "now let's all get back to work, shall we?"

There were some grumblings about the tea break being cut short but very soon almost the whole shift had returned to their duties.

"You sure know how to cut a tea break short, Will," said Marie as she walked past him and out into the corridor, leaving just him, John and Sally in the staff room.

"I guess I'd better get back to it," said Will light-heartedly, hoping to avoid the inevitable lecture that he knew he was going to get from Sally.

"Yes, me too," echoed John, the same thought running through his mind.

"Just a moment you two," said Sally, her voice carrying the hard edge of a good-natured boss pushed to do something they hate.

The two men, who a moment before had been ready to trade blows looked at each other and sighed in mutual resignation of their fate and turned to face the music.

"Do I have to say how stupid you two are, or can you figure it out for yourselves?"

"I'm," John started to say but could not finish his sentence before Sally interrupted him.

"Save it, John, I'm not interested. The pair of you should have known better. Now listen very carefully, I'm going let it go this time. But trust me when I say that another display like the one I just witnessed means the pair of you can look for another place to work. Do you understand me?"

The two men now joined by that well-known telepathy of fools in trouble, simply nodded their answer.

"Good, now if I were you, I would get back to work."

Both John and Will took their cue to leave eagerly and headed for the door as quickly as their bruised egos would allow. Once outside the staff room John turned to Will and said, "I'm sorry I got out of hand, Will, it was stupid of me."

"Me too," said Will holding out his hand again. "No hard feelings?"

This time John took the offered hand willingly and shook it with meaning.

"No, no hard feelings, it's just this place, it makes me jumpy."

"I know what you mean, John, it creeps me out as well sometimes."

As the two men parted company to go about their duties John said, "You're alright Will, so please listen. There never was any initiation ceremony planned for you. No one who works here for long would want to play tricks about ghosts."

"Please, John, you're not going to tell me that this place is haunted are you."

"I'm not going to tell you, anything son. But I will give you a little advice if you'll take it."

"Go on then."

"While you're here at night," said John, the smile slipping from his face, "don't fall asleep."

Before Will could ask John what he meant Sally came out of the staff room and said, "You two still here?"

"No, Sally," Will said turning and walking quickly down the corridor, "I'm not here at all."

Sally waited until Will was out of sight before she let herself have a slight smile at the young man's expense. He'd done well to not punch John and she realised it had taken a lot for him to be the bigger man and hold his hand out first. She decided she liked the newest member of staff.

Will carried on with his shift quietly for the next two hours, emptying wastebaskets, replacing toilet paper, cleaning, dusting, and doing another thousand and one jobs that needed to be done so that Crabtree Lodge ran smoothly. It was while he was sweeping the floor in the old schoolroom that Marie, at last, managed to catch up with him.

"What did Sally say?" she asked as she handed him a cup of instant coffee that she had managed to sneak out of the staff room for him.

Will took the coffee and sipped at it gratefully before he answered.

"Only what you would have expected. She chewed us out and told us how stupid we were."

"Lucky for you it was Sally and not Molly who was working tonight."

"Why?" Will asked as he sat down on an old packing crate.

"Because Molly would have sacked you both on the spot, she's a real one for following all the rules and regulations. But Sally's more like one of us."

"Marie," Will said, taking another sip of his coffee, "if I ask you a serious question will you answer it?"

"I'll try," Marie said, her smile fading a little when she saw that Will wasn't joking.

"When John and I left the staff room before he walked off, he told me to never go to sleep in this place. Do you know what he means?"

Marie hesitated for a moment unsure what to say. She had started too really like Will but didn't want to get involved in all the superstition that revolved around Crabtree Lodge. The expression on Will's face told her that he wasn't going to settle for anything but a straight answer.

"Yes, Will I do, but I don't believe any of it."

Will didn't say anything he just sipped at his coffee and waited for her to continue.

"Some of the older staff say that this place gives you nightmares. And I don't mean the kind where you're naked walking down the street or something that you can't remember when you wake up. I mean nightmares that stay with you and follow you about all day and make you afraid to ever go to sleep again."

"That sounds like a cure for constipation," Will said as he finished his coffee. "Have you ever fallen asleep here?"

"No, I haven't, and I don't intend to. This place gives me the creeps. It's the last place I would want to catch forty winks."

"Do you know anyone who has fallen asleep here?"

"Only Bruno, he used to do your job but asked for a transfer to the kitchens after his first week."

"A week, that's not long."

"It's longer than most."

Will caught the subtle undertone in Marie's voice and asked, "Is there something I should know about this job Marie?"

"Only that as of yesterday, you are the longest-serving night porter in years,"

"But that's insane; I've only been here three weeks.

"Let me tell you, Will, we've had people that have left inside three days one guy was gone inside two hours."

"But that's mad," Will said standing up and putting his now empty cup on the crate beside him. "Are you saying that there's something in Crabtree Lodge so scary that people won't work here?"

"I'm not saying anything like that. I like working here and I've never seen or heard anything to suggest there is anything out of the ordinary going on. But some people would be very eager to tell you differently if you let them."

"You've got to admit it's intriguing."

"Not for me. For me this is just a place to pay the bills, I don't want to know anything more than that thank you."

As Marie walked off Will blurted out the question he had been planning to ask all night but had just not found the courage.

"It's my sister's birthday at the weekend and she's having a party; do you fancy coming?"

Marie stopped, turned and looked Will slowly up and down. For a moment Will thought she was going to say no then she smiled and said, "Yes ok, why not?"

Will watched her walk away and as he picked up his broom, he said to himself, "A fight, a date, and a ghost story. Not a bad night Will, not a bad night at all."

Chapter Six

The next day, Will got into work early to go and see if he could meet Bruno and ask him about his experiences with Crabtree Lodge.

The lodge in the daytime was a stark contrast to the lodge at night. He couldn't help but notice that even the building itself looked somehow different; no longer threatening, with a warm, cosy feeling to it. He would never have noticed anything if he hadn't worked nights. It was like holding up two pieces of paper which had been painted different shades of the same colour. Separately they looked the same but held side by side the contrast was striking.

Will was also struck by how different the day staff seemed; just as friendly, most of them nodding hello as Will walked through the large, oak doors of the front entrance, but without that slight sense of unease that the night staff seemed to have about them. Something that he hadn't noticed until it wasn't there. Also, the residents seemed happier, more alive and vibrant. As Will walked through the lodge the whole atmosphere of the place was different. Kinder, more caring. Not that the night staff were unkind or uncaring, it was more the building itself that had changed.

Will walked through to the rear of the lodge where the kitchens were located.

"Hello, Will," said Amanda, the catering manager, as Will walked into the large busy kitchen. "What brings you to us?"

"Hi, Amanda," Will said, smiling at the small middle-aged woman who ran the kitchen. "Just popped in a bit early is all, is Bruno about?"

"Ah, Bruno. I thought you might be here sooner or later. Almost all of you night workers come to see him."

Amanda laughed when she saw the look of astonishment on Will's face.

"He's over there," she said as she pointed across the kitchen to a large, coloured man in chef's whites.

"Thanks, Amanda," Will said as he started across the busy kitchen.

Just as he was about to introduce himself to Bruno, the big man said, "Hello, Will,"

"You know me?"

"I know you're the new night porter," Bruno said turning to face the smaller man, "and I know why you're here. You want to ask me about when I was the night porter don't you?"

"I do if you don't mind?"

"I don't, but once we've talked you might. I'm due a break in about ten minutes so if you wait for me outside, we can talk then."

Will looked at Bruno, trying to see if the man was playing with him. But nothing in the other man's face or body language suggested anything other than honesty.

"Ok, then I'll meet you outside."

A little over fifteen minutes later Bruno came to the back door of the kitchen where Will was waiting.

"Alright," said the big man as he stepped outside, "what do you want to know?"

At first, Will was at a loss for what to say. All the questions that he'd wanted to ask now seemed more than a little childish, especially now when he'd walked through the place during the height of the day.

Bruno smiled when he saw the younger man hesitate, "It's a strange job being a night porter here isn't it?"

"I guess you could say that," smiled Will, "but no one will tell me anything about this place. It's like there's some dark secret that everyone's afraid to speak about."

"I don't know about dark secrets, but it's not the nicest place I've ever spent a night and that's for sure."

"Is this place haunted, Bruno?"

"Yes, it is. Now, do you feel any better for the knowledge?"

"No, not really. Can you tell me anymore?"

"A lot, if you think you're up to it."

For the next half hour, Bruno talked, and Will listened to the gruesome story of Crabtree Lodge and its founder, Sir Otto Crabtree.

Will heard how Otto Crabtree opened the lodge as a consumption hospital for children. He used his fortune to build the place and funded it with contributions from a host of rich friends. Otto was venerated in the press and the local community as a pillar of society and as a forward thinker in medicine and childcare. But Otto's life was cut short.

He seemed to have suffered a heart attack on the very night that the capstone was to be placed above the main entrance of the building. The works foreman found him slumped over the Latin-inscribed stone when he arrived for work that morning.

At first, the building work was halted but once Otto's will was read it was clear that the man had realised that he was ill and made provisions in case this very thing happened. He had left clear instructions that in the event of his death the building should be finished, and the children should be cared for.

This one last magnanimous gesture reached the ear of the new king. And Otto was posthumously knighted for his humanitarian efforts. All of this sounded alright to Will. In an age where the rich only truly cared about themselves and where little lost orphans were the lowest of the low this one man had stood out as a shining beacon of what could be possible if only people cared. But then Bruno's story started to take a darker turn. The hospital soon started to build a reputation for quick staff turnover and a high mortality rate. Even at a time where jobs were short and life was sometimes even shorter, Crabtree Lodge stood out.

In the local pub when the night drew in and the wind and rain lashed at the windows; talk would turn to what walked the halls of the lodge late at night. People would buy drinks for the tight-lipped staff to get them to talk about what they had seen. Sometimes, just sometimes, when the mood was right and a member of staff from the lodge had drunk enough to loosen their tongue, they would talk. Always in a whisper and always with a surreptitious glance over their shoulder.

They would speak of a dark shadow that lurked near the dying, waiting for them, some would say even feeding off them. They would talk about how afraid the children were once the sun went down. How the terminally ill would cry when the lights were turned off and ask staff to stay with them so the man would not come.

When these poor unfortunates were asked who the man was none of them could say, but each one of their descriptions was eerily similar. All the children described the same man: Sir Otto Crabtree.

"That's a hell of a story Bruno," Will said once the other man had finished speaking, "but you can't tell me that you believe all that. I mean it's just so farfetched."

"Yes, that's what I thought when I heard it. That is until I fell asleep here one night. The next day I asked for a transfer to days and moved into the kitchens. It's less money to be sure, but I tell you, brother, money isn't everything."

"You fell asleep, what can be so bad about that?"

"I met Phillip Green," said Bruno softly, almost as if he was afraid to be overheard.

"Phillip Green, who's he?"

"Phillip Green was the first person to die here at the lodge," Bruno said staring Will directly in the eye daring him to laugh.

Will could see the seriousness in the other man's eyes. This was no joke, no wind-up. Bruno truly believed what he was saying. The only thing Will could do was wait for the other man to continue.

"It was my second week as the night porter that it happened. I'd had a wild day off and not had a moment to get any sleep, so by the time I got to work I was shattered. But work's work as you know so I settled in for a long hard shift and just tried to get through it. By about three in the morning the day had caught up with me, and I was more like a zombie than a man, so I decided to take a nap. You know, just to liven myself up a little. I found an unoccupied room at the end of the first floor and settled down. That was when it happened."

"What happened?"

"I had only just closed my eyes when the door slammed open and a young boy rushed in and hid behind the chair that sat in one corner. I was so tired that I didn't think how strange it was that a boy of what could only have been nine or ten was running around a nursing home. Or why he was there so late at night. The only thing I did was say hello."

"Did he answer you?"

"Yes, he did, but I wish he hadn't. The fear in that young voice is something I'm going to carry with me for a very long time."

"What did he say?"

"It's been well over a year since that night Will, but I remember his words as if it was yesterday. 'Help me,' he said, 'please help me. He's coming and I can't go through this again.' And I know what you're going to say, Will. Who was he talking about?"

Will nodded in reply unsure how else to answer.

"It was Otto, Will, the man himself, as large as life. I've never seen anything like it before, and I pray I never see anything like it again. This giant of a man came striding into the room laughing if you could call it laughing. I could only say that if the devil ever laughed then it would have sounded like that. And he spoke to me. He turned and looked at me, and he spoke. And his voice, it was like being slapped across the face by a gauntlet."

"What did he say?" Will asked, his imagination flaming with the images that Bruno was creating.

"'You're a lucky man,' he said as he pointed a finger at me," Bruno answered, pointing his finger at Will in imitation of the ghostly Otto. "'It's the boy I want tonight, but maybe when you sleep again, I will come for you.' Then still laughing he grabbed the chair, threw it across the room, and picked up the boy in his outstretched arms. It was horrible, the boy screaming and the man laughing. And then the worst thing of all happened. Otto opened his mouth and breathed in deeply. As soon as he did that the boy stopped screaming and just hung there limp like a puppet with its strings cut, and a small silver slither of something came out of his body and into Otto's mouth. It was like he was feeding off him or something. And that was when I woke up. I quit the job that morning and transferred here."

"That's a hell of a story Bruno, but you can't believe it was anything more than a nightmare, can you?"

"I'll believe what I want thanks. You weren't there, you didn't see that poor boy's face or hear his screams and you didn't see that monster pick him up and drain that weird energy from him. I did and dream or not I wasn't going to take a chance that it would be me next time."

"But even so..."

"I've heard it all before, Will, but the fact is that no one who falls asleep doing your job is still working at the lodge the next day. And the chair in the room that Bruno threw across the room that was smashed when I woke up. So, you decide what you want, that's up to you, but I'm never here at sundown and I never will be."

Once Bruno stopped talking an awkward silence started to grow between them. Will found it hard to believe such a fantastic story yet he could see that Bruno truly believed everything he was saying.

"Well, Bruno," Will said at last, "thanks for taking the time to see me, I do appreciate it."

"No problem, man. I know you don't believe me but that's OK, no one ever does. But there is one way to see for yourself you know."

"Oh yes, what's that?"

"It's simple. Just go to sleep inside the lodge."

Chapter Seven

After Will finished his conversation with Bruno he went to the staff room, made himself a coffee, and sat in the deck chair to think about what the chef had told him.

"It can't be true," he said to the empty room as he sipped at his steaming drink. "It just can't be."

"But what if it is?" said a small voice from the back of his mind. "What if Bruno was telling the truth and this place is alive with ghosts and monsters?"

Will tried his best to ignore the voice, but he couldn't. It stayed in his mind stuck there like an itch he could not scratch. As he sat there trying to digest all that he had been told, Marie walked into the staff room

"You're early," she said as she saw him sitting in the deck chair.

"Oh hello," Will said absentmindedly as he nursed his coffee.

"Are you alright, Will?"

"What? Oh, sorry, Marie, yes, I'm ok. I've just got a lot on my mind."

"Want to talk about it?"

Will thought for a moment. He wanted to tell Marie what Bruno had told him, but he was afraid that this woman he was starting to have some real feelings for would think he was just some kind of fruitcake and terminate their blossoming romance.

"Hey, come on," Marie said when she saw Will's hesitation. "This is me you know."

"Alright, I'll tell you. But please don't laugh."

Marie didn't reply, she just sat there looking at Will and sipping at her coffee.

"I'm here early because I wanted to have a chat with Bruno. He used to be the night porter here."

"Yes, I know, Bruno's an old friend of mine."

"I wanted to hear what he had to say about this place. To be honest he's kind of shaken me up a bit."

"Yes, quite a tale he tells, isn't it?"

"You've heard it?"

"Of course I have, what part of 'he's an old friend' didn't you understand?"

Normally Will would have responded in kind to Marie's sarcasm, but he had become more than a little wrapped up in Bruno's story.

"Do you believe him?" he asked.

At first, Marie was going to answer with her best sarcastic tone. But then she saw something in Will's eyes that made her change her mind.

"To be honest I'm not sure. This is an odd place and if you're alone at night then perhaps your imagination could get away from you. But ghosts and monsters? I think I'm a little too old for all that. And as I've told you before, I've never seen anything like that for as long as I've worked here."

"But you've never fallen asleep here."

"No, I've not, and I never intend to. I've heard that old story from Bruno on more than one occasion, and even though I don't believe any of it I can't say that it didn't seriously creeps me out."

"Do you know anyone else who has slept here on their shift?"

Marie didn't answer right away she just looked down at the ground and sipped at her coffee.

"Marie," Will prompted.

"Yes OK," Marie said, her voice full of irritation.

"What's the matter?"

"You'll hear this sooner or later from someone so you might as well hear it from me."

"Hear what?"

Marie hesitated a moment longer. "Everyone who falls asleep here at night leaves the next day. I've been here five years and in all that time there have been no exceptions. They all leave, and they all leave in one hell of a hurry."

"What, all of them?"

"Yes, everyone."

"But that's incredible."

"Look Will, can we change the subject? All this talk of ghosts and stuff makes me very uncomfortable."

Will could see how stressed Marie was becoming. The last thing he wanted to do was upset her, so despite his eagerness to hear more he said, "Yes, of course, I'm sorry I didn't mean to upset you."

"That's OK," Marie said, visibly relaxing now that they were off the subject of the lodge's more permanent residents, "anyway, I'm glad I found you're here so early because there's something I want to ask you."

"Really?" said Will, all thoughts of ghosts pushed from his mind by the inflexion in Marie's voice.

"Well, as you've invited me to your sister's birthday party, I want to invite you to my friend's eclipse party."

"Eclipse party? What's that?"

"You're joking, right? My God Will where have you been, living under a rock? You know, the eclipse? The solar eclipse, the first total eclipse in this part of the country for a hundred and ten years?"

"Sorry, I don't know anything about it. I guess I don't pay much attention to the news."

Will hated the news or anything like it. The moment it came on the T.V. or radio he would change the channel. He also never bought newspapers or magazines. He was well and truly a media virgin.

"Even if you don't know about it it's still going to be a great party. So do you want to come?"

"Yes, of course, I do."

"Great," Marie said, smiling back at him relieved.

It wasn't her style to ask a man to go anywhere, but with Will, it felt different somehow. She didn't want to seem pushy, but by the same turn, she didn't want to seem too aloof.

"Anyway," she said, far more nonchalantly than she felt, "I've got work to do. See you at tea break?"

"Yes, see you then."

As soon as she was outside in the corridor Marie leaned against the wall, shut her eyes and let out a huge, quiet sigh.

"What's the matter with you?" she said to the empty corridor, "you're not fourteen and he's not your first boyfriend, not by a long way. You've not even kissed him yet."

At the thought of Will's lips on hers, Marie felt her heart start to race.

"Come on," Marie said to the still empty corridor. "Pull yourself together and get some work done."

As she went off to start her shift Marie would have been surprised to know that Will was having almost the same conversation with himself in the staff room.

The first part of Will's shift passed swiftly and before he knew it, he was back in the staff room enjoying his tea break and the company of Marie and the others. But all too soon his break was over, and he found himself alone again, cleaning.

He was in the old school room when he started to feel like someone was watching him. Normally he liked the schoolroom but tonight no matter how hard he tried he could not shake the feeling of a pair of eyes boring into the back of his neck.

"Come on," Will said softly, as he stopped his work to look around the long-disused room. "It's just your imagination."

"Are you sure?" said an unfamiliar voice from behind him.

Will felt his feet leave the floor as a jolt of fear raced through him. He didn't know what to expect as he spun around, but the sight of the old and frail-looking Joan standing there smiling sweetly at him in her housecoat and pink fluffy slippers was just about the last thing.

"Joan, what are you doing here?"

"I've been asked to speak to you, Will," Joan said in a whisper as she looked first over one shoulder, and then the other.

"OK then, who asked you to speak to me?"

"Phillip did. He and the others are convinced that you're the one."

"The one what, Joan? And who's Phillip?"

"There you are, Joan," Marie said from the doorway of the schoolroom, "everyone's been looking for you."

Before Marie crossed the space between them Joan stepped forward and whispered urgently to Will.

"Please come to my room in an hour."

"Come on then, Joan," Marie said good-naturedly as she put her arm gently around the old woman's shoulders, "let's get you back to your room and leave Will to get on with his work."

"Alright, dear," Joan said, her voice losing its intelligence to be replaced by what Will realised to be a fake shambling quiver.

"Sorry about this, Will," Marie said as she led Joan away. "Joan rarely leaves her room at night. I hope she didn't scare you."

"No, it's fine," Will said trying his best to make light of this very strange situation, "only a mild heart attack this time."

"That's OK then," Marie said, her sense of humour as dry as ever.

As Will watched Marie escort, Joan, back to her room the old woman raised her hand behind her and clenched her fist but left her index finger pointing out. Will saw the gesture and knew what it implied.

"Ok, Joan," he said softly to himself, "one hour."

An hour later Will was standing outside Joan's room. He was aware of what he was about to do because if anyone should find him in a female patient's room, alone, in the early hours of the morning they would reach only one conclusion, and they would reach it at light speed. But curiosity got the better of him, and he had to know what Joan wanted to say.

Just as he was about to knock softly on her door Joan's voice drifted through it. "Come in, Will."

"OK," said Will as he reached for the handle, "that's not scary."

Will opened the door to Joan's room and went in quickly before anyone saw him.

"Hello," Joan said, gone was the dithering old lady and in her place sat a woman whose eyes shone with intelligence and whose voice was strong and full of authority.

"Joan?" Will asked, unsure for a moment if the woman sitting across from him was, in fact, the woman that he had met on his first day.

"Almost," said Joan enigmatically, as she sat forward and smiled.

"OK," Will said uncertainly, realising that he was alone with someone who he didn't know at all, and who now seemed more than a little unhinged, "are you alright, Joan?"

"I'm fine, Will. I'm sorry if I scared you. Sometimes I forget how it must look when I'm like this. Please take a seat we have a lot to talk about."

Will took a straight-backed chair from beside the closed door, sat down, and waited for the old woman to start to talk.

Chapter Eight

"This might be a little hard for you to believe, Will," Joan said after a moment's pause, "but please bear with me and let me finish, OK?"

"OK."

"The woman you see sitting here in front of you is not the Joan that you met on your first day. That poor woman is frail, and her mind is quite weak and wanders away from her often. I, on the other hand, am the Joan that might have been had the ravages of time been somewhat kinder than they have been."

Before Will could say anything, Joan held up her hand, "please, Will, I know how this sounds, but let me finish. I can prove all that I'm saying, I promise."

Will thought for a moment. What he had just heard did indeed sound very strange but then no stranger than what he had heard from Bruno, and certainly no stranger than the image of a small boy moving about in a picture.

"Alright, Joan, I'll hear you out."

"Thank you," Joan said, smiling as she sat back in her chair, "you are the first person who has come to this place that might just be able to help them."

Will could feel the question of whom building up behind his teeth, but he fought the impulse to ask and let Joan continue to talk.

"First let me explain myself. I am Joan but my dementia for the moment has been suppressed so that I can speak on behalf of those who can't speak for themselves, but I must be quick because we can't let him know that we are talking."

"You mean Otto, don't you?"

As soon as Will mentioned the lodge's founder the lights in the room flickered and a small picture that had been resting on Joan's night table fell to the floor.

"Please, Will, don't mention his name. It makes them so nervous."

"Joan, I don't mean to interrupt but who are you talking about? Who are they?"

"They, Will," Joan said, a look of utter sadness passing across her old and careworn face, "are the souls of the poor unfortunate children that he's trapped in this godforsaken place, and before you ask, I'm not talking about ghosts. Ghosts are just the afterimage of something that's gone before. What I'm talking about is the soul. That part of us that goes on once this suit of flesh and bone that we wear has run its course."

"But what has all this got to do with me? What can I do?"

"They see something in you, Will, something that they have not seen in anyone for a long time."

"What, Joan? What do they see in me? I'm a nobody."

"No, Will, you're not. You're a dreamer, a romantic. In a world of cynics, you want to believe. You try to be a good man when it might be easier to be bad or apathetic. You search for love in a world where that very word sometimes loses all its meaning. You are a man out of your time. This is what they see in you, Will. They see a champion."

For a moment Will was lost for words. As far as he knew he was none of the things that Joan had said, and he was the farthest thing from a champion that he could imagine. He hated to fight. The few fights that he had been in, he had always come out second. He wasn't brave or anything like it. He avoided trouble whenever he could.

"I'm sorry, Joan but I think you've got the wrong man."

"Take my hand," Joan said, holding out her small child-like hand, "take my hand and let them speak to you themselves."

Before he knew what he was doing Will was crossing Joan's small room, his hand outstretched ready to grasp hers. But just before his hand touched hers Will seemed to come to his senses and snatched his hand back.

"Hang on a minute, what the hell just happened?"

"I'm sorry," Joan said lowering her hand so that it rested in her lap, "they can be quite impatient sometimes."

"You mean they made me walk over to you?"

"I'm afraid so, but it won't happen again I can assure you. They are just eager to meet you. But it must be your choice Will and yours alone. So will you take my hand?"

Will looked down as Joan once more offered her hand out to him. He knew he could just turn around and walk away. No one would blame him, even if they knew, but something inside him just would not let him leave. What if all this was true and there were souls trapped here in Crabtree Lodge? Could he look at himself each morning as he washed, knowing that he had just turned his back on them without even trying to help?

He knew that he couldn't, and with a nervous smile, he reached out and took the old woman's hand. The moment his hand touched hers the room seemed to dim and fall away, and for a moment Will thought he was going to pass out.

"Hello Will," said a voice from in front of him.

At first, Will couldn't see who had spoken but as his vision cleared, he saw, standing just behind Joan, a tall thin woman in a long black dress with a high white collar. He knew he should have been scared out of his wits by this woman's sudden appearance, but for some reason, he wasn't. There was something about her, something caring. It dawned on Will that she was dressed like a nurse.

"Hello," Will said in reply.

"My name's Martha Allen, Will. I was once the matron here at Crabtree Lodge."

"You mean you're a ghost?"

"In a way, I suppose I am, but in another, not at all."

"I don't understand"

"It's alright Will, it's not important who I am. What is important is that you help these poor unfortunates."

As she said this Martha tilted her head to the left. Will's eyes followed her gesture. At first, he could only make out shadows in the corner of the room, but then ever so slowly these shadows solidified into the forms of half a dozen small children, four boys and two girls. The children gathered around Martha's legs and looked at Will.

"These are the souls of the children that Otto Crabtree has trapped here, they need your help, Will. What do you say?"

Will looked at the expectant faces of the children that now stood in front of him. Their desperation pulled at him. These poor innocents had been used and abused repeatedly to keep a monster alive and entertained for over a hundred years, and if he did not help then their nightmare would go on unabated for who knew how long.

Will didn't know what he could do for them, but he did know that if he didn't try and help then their young faces would swim in his imagination for the rest of his life.

"Yes, I will," he said as he looked at Martha and the children. "I'll help."

The look of joy and hope that overcame the children in front of him almost broke Will's heart. One of them, the youngest of the group by the look of her, stepped forward and said, quite simply, "Thank you."

The young girl's voice was so full of gratitude that Will could not help kneeling so that he could look her in the eyes.

"What's your name, sweetheart?"

"Margery, sir," said the small girl with a curtsey, her eyes downcast and her voice sounding ever so small.

"Please, Margery, don't call me sir. My name's Will."

Margery looked up at Martha before she said anything.

"Yes, dear," Martha said with a smile, "it's OK, go ahead."

Margery looked back at Will and said softly, "Thank you, Will."

As Will stood up a movement in the shadows on the far side of the room caught his eye. As he watched another child materialised, a boy Will recognized instantly. He'd been seeing him every day since he first arrived at Crabtree Lodge. This was the boy looking out from the photograph that hung just inside the main doors.

Will knew without asking that this must be Phillip Green before Will could say anything, the newcomer ran up to Martha and whispered urgently.

"Martha, he's coming."

As soon as these words were out of the boy's mouth the other children ran for the shadows and disappeared.

"What's happening?" Will asked, "who's coming?"

"It's Otto," Martha answered as she cast her eyes about the room, "he's on his way here. He can't find us together Will. He mustn't know that you know what's going on. If he had any idea, he would destroy you and the children would be lost."

"What do you want me to do?"

"Leave now. Phillip here will contact you soon."

"Hello Will," said the young boy that had arrived last in the room.

"Hello Phillip," Will said, liking the boy immediately.

"We have to leave Martha," Phillip said, "he's almost here, I can feel him."

"We have to go, Will," Martha said, her voice tinged with genuine fear.

Will watched as the two figures in front of him melted into the shadows. They faded and faded until there was just him and Joan in the room again.

Will looked down at the old woman in front of him. Without Martha's influence, she was just a poor individual locked inside her senility. Suddenly Joan looked up, her eyes cleared for a moment, and she hissed, "Run."

This shocked Will into movement, and he was on the other side of the door almost before he knew it. As he stood there in the darkened corridor, he felt a terrible presence flow through the door, and he knew that Otto Crabtree was now only inches away from him. Will wanted to run but something held him there and despite himself, he pressed his ear against the cold wood of the door to try and hear if anything was being said on the other side.

At first, he couldn't hear anything other than Joan mumbling, but suddenly, for the first time outside of his dream, he heard the cold and terrible voice of Otto Crabtree shouting.

"DON'T TELL THEM ANYTHING ABOUT US, JOAN."

Will couldn't help himself; he fled down the corridor, Otto's voice resounding in his ears. Will didn't stop running until he reached the staff room and it was with a sigh of relief that he opened the door and saw Marie filling the kettle in preparation for the last tea break of the shift.

"Are you alright Will?" she asked when she saw the look on his face.

"I've been better," Will said as he shut the door behind him and welcomed the normality that the staff room offered.

Chapter Nine

"What's happened, Will?" Marie asked as she put down the steaming kettle and walked over to him.

Will knew there was no way he could tell her what had just happened; she would think he was making fun of her. But he had to tell her something, and he had to do it before anyone else turned up for their tea break.

"I've just got a bit freaked out tonight, I guess all that talk of ghosts and stuff caught up with me. I was in the schoolroom and for the life of me I could have sworn I saw something moving in the shadows."

Marie looked at Will for a long moment before she replied. She could see that he was scared so she bit back the sarcasm that was trying its best to escape, smiled, and said, "Don't worry. This place gets to everyone sooner or later. Come on let's get you a cup of tea."

Will breathed a small sigh of relief as Marie turned around and poured the boiling water into the oversized teapot that stood on the table. To add fuel to his deception he said, "You won't say anything, will you? If anyone hears about this, I'm never going to live it down."

"No of course not, though it's tempting I must say. So, if you want me to keep it a secret then you had best be nice to me."

"I can do that. Where would you like me to start?"

"You can finish making this tea," Marie said, sitting down in one of the armchairs, "and I'll see what else I can come up with."

As he poured out the tea, the rest of the night shift arrived for their break. Surrounded by people again Will started to relax. The fear that had grabbed hold of him when he heard that terrible voice was slipping away and he started to think about what happened in Joan's room. However insane it might sound to anyone else those events had happened. There was a monster walking the halls of Crabtree Lodge and there were ghosts in the world. As these thoughts flew through his mind a sudden alarm cut through his thoughts and set the whole room into motion.

"It's Joan," Sally said urgently as she looked at the flashing light on the nurse's board.

Nothing more was said, nothing more was needed. Sally had trained her shift well and everyone knew what to do. Within seconds the nurses were gone; one going for the resuscitation equipment and the others heading directly for Joan's room. The only two people left in the room were Will and John.

"What's going on?" Will asked the older man.

"It's a crash."

"A crash, what's that?"

"Each patient has a panic button that they wear around their necks at night so that if they fall or something then they press that and the whole nursing staff respond, just like you saw them do now, and before you ask, all the patients know that it's only to be used in a real emergency."

"What do we do?"

"We stay out of the way and let the nurses do their job. Don't let them know I said this, but those people are just about the best I've ever worked with."

The two men drank their tea in silence after that, each of them wondering what was going on. Will, because of what he had just seen in the old lady's room and John because, despite the grouchy image he projected, he liked the patients who lived at the lodge, Joan in particular.

"I'd best get on," John said as he put his empty cup in the sink, "and you'd best do the same. There's no point waiting here, they could be gone for the rest of the shift. We'll find out soon enough what's happened."

Then just like that Will was alone. He knew he should go back to work like John, but he was loathed to leave the imagined safety of the staff room. The fact that it had been Joan's panic button that had gone off could not have been a coincidence. Something had happened to the old woman because she had tried to help the ghosts trapped at the lodge. And if something had happened to Joan, didn't that mean that something could happen to him as well?

"You can't hide in here," he said aloud, trying to find comfort in the sound of his voice.

"We wouldn't blame you if you did, Will," Martha said as she stepped out of the shadows that gathered beside the group of old lockers.

In only a few short hours Will had gone from believing that ghosts and spectres were the things of children's imaginations to total acceptance of them, so without a trace of shock in his voice he said, "What happened to Joan, Martha?"

"She's dead," Martha answered softly, her voice conveying the sadness that filled her heart.

"Dead? How can she be dead?"

"It was Otto. He lives off the children but sometimes he will terrorise a patient for fun. But I think that this time there was more to it. I think Otto knows that we are planning something and that Joan was involved so he killed her. But all the nurses will find is a poor old woman whose heart gave out."

"I'm not sure I'm cut out for this."

"You must be. There is no one else."

"But what can I do? How can I stop something like Otto?"

"You don't have to stop him, Will, all you have to do is find his soul."

"His soul? How on earth do I do that?"

As he spoke Will noticed that Martha didn't seem to be listening to him, rather her attention seemed to be occupied by something else.

"What the matter, Martha?"

"Someone's coming I have to go."

Will watched in astonishment as Martha once more started to fade before his eyes, and just before she vanished completely, she said, "Tell no one about us, no one. We believe that someone here is helping Otto, working with him and protecting him. So please tell no one. Trust no one."

Before Will could ask any more questions Martha was gone.

The next moment the staff room door opened, and Marie and Sally walked slowly into the room.

"Make us a tea, Will," Sally said sadly as she slumped down into one of the armchairs.

"What happened?"

"Joan's dead, Will," Marie said as she went and sat down beside Sally.

"Oh," Will said, unsure what he should say or even if he should act surprised, but neither of the two women noticed anything out of the ordinary. They were both still shocked by Joan's sudden demise. Neither had expected anything was wrong with the lovely old woman but they both knew that no matter how healthy someone looked when they were as old as she had been then death could take them any time.

Knowing this did not make it any easier to bear. Both Sally and Marie tried their best to avoid attachments with their older patients, but occasionally, one would sneak in under their defences and this time that one had been Joan.

For the next few moments, silence filled the staff room. Will occupied himself making tea for the two nurses. He knew he should ask them what had happened to Joan, but he didn't want them to suspect that he knew anything about what had happened, and God forbid they should find out that he had been in the old lady's room mere minutes before she had died.

"What happened to her, Marie?" he asked as compassionately as he could, handing over the steaming cups of tea.

"It looks like it was her heart, but she must have been in terrible pain at the end. The look on her poor face was horrible."

"I'm so sorry," Will said, feeling real sympathy for the beautiful young woman sitting in front of him. "Is there anything I can do?"

"You can take, Marie home, Will," Sally said, answering for her younger colleague.

"I can't go home," Marie said.

"Yes, you can dear, you were close to Joan and there's nothing left here to do apart from the paperwork and to wait for the doctor. So go home, get some rest, and I will see you tomorrow."

"But, Sally," Marie said, protesting again.

"No buts, Marie, go home."

Marie knew there was no arguing with the head nurse when she had that tone in her voice, so graciously she said, "OK, thank you."

"Good, and Will, once you drop Marie off, I don't think there's much point you coming back, so I'll see you tomorrow as well."

"Thanks, Sally," Will said, surprised at getting almost half his shift off.

A few minutes later Will and Marie were walking across the dark and empty parking lot of Crabtree Lodge.

"I am sorry about Joan," Will said, unsure if he should put his arm around her or not.

"Thanks, I knew this was going to happen sooner or later. Joan was very old. I just wish that she hadn't suffered so much."

"But you said it was her heart. I thought that kind of thing happened almost at once."

"Mostly it does," Marie agreed, taking hold of Will's arm and solving his dilemma by putting it around her shoulder, "but with Joan it was different."

"Different?"

"It was her face; she looked so terrified. She must have been so scared and with her senility, she couldn't have known what was happening to her. It looked like she lived her last few moments of life in total terror. I can't think of a more horrible way to go."

At that moment Will wanted to tell Marie everything that had happened that evening. To tell her that Joan had known what was happening to her and to say that she had been murdered. But Martha's words drifted back to him.

"It can't be Marie," Will thought as he looked at the woman beside him. "It can't be."

"You OK, Will?" Marie asked when she noticed how deep in thought he was.

"Yes, I'm fine, just thinking about Joan."

"Well don't do that," Marie said as she got into the passenger seat of Will's car. "Just take me home."

As he started the car Will said, "So where is home?"

"It's across town. If you go through the town centre, I'll direct you from there."

The pair of them drove in silence through the early morning streets, each of them wrapped in their own thoughts. At last, Will pulled up outside the large, rambling building that housed Marie's flat.

"Thanks, Will, I don't think I could have driven myself home tonight."

"No problem," Will said, unsure if he wanted her to invite him in or not. It had been such a strange and disturbing night that he wanted to go home but he knew that if she did invite him in, he would have to go.

"I would invite you in, but I just want to be alone now. You understand, don't you?"

"Yes of course I do," Will said feeling both relief and disappointment at the same time, "you don't have to explain."

Marie leaned over and brushed her lips gently against Will's. He felt as if a sudden electric charge had been passed through his body.

"Can you pick me up tonight?" she said as she got out of the car, her face as red as Will's. "My car's still at the lodge."

"Err yes, of course, I can."

"See you at eight then," Marie said as she shut the door and walked up the small set of steps that led to her front door.

Will watched her until she had vanished from sight. Then with a small sigh, he pulled away and started his journey home.

Chapter Ten

Will arrived home just as the new day's sun rose lazily into the morning sky. The events of the night had left him physically and mentally drained and it was with a grateful sigh that he undressed and crawled into bed. He was asleep almost before he had turned out the light.

"Will, Will," said a voice beside his bed, rousing him from his dreamless sleep.

Will sat up in bed, casting his eyes about the sun-dappled room for the owner of the voice that had woken him.

"Who's there?" he said, real fear running up his spine.

"It's alright," Martha said as she stepped out of the shadows that had gathered beside his wardrobe for protection from the unforgiving sun.

"Martha," Will said, shocked to see the nurse there in his home, "I don't understand, how can you be here?"

"I'm not here, at least not as you mean it. You're still asleep. This is a dream, but a dream of my making."

"What are you talking about?" Will said as he swung his legs out of bed and stood up, "I'm not dreaming, I'm awake."

"Are you sure?" Martha said as she nodded past him to his bed.

Will turned slowly to see himself sleeping peacefully.

"OK, that's not creepy."

"I need to tell you things Will, show you things so that you can realise that coming to us was no accident. We have waited a long time for your return."

"What do you mean return?"

"Come with me," Martha said as she walked through the open bedroom door, "and I will explain everything."

Will took one more look at himself asleep in his bed and followed the nurse through the doorway, straight into the corridors of Crabtree

Lodge. Not the corridors that he was used too, these were brand new, with glistening paint and woodwork that looked as if the varnish had only now dried.

"Yes," Martha said answering his unspoken question, "this is the lodge as it was when it was new. Isn't it beautiful?"

Will had to admit that it was. There was something noble about the place that did not exist as he knew it. It felt like a place a person could come to when they were in pain and be cared for, a place of succour and rest.

"This was once a truly amazing place," Martha said, wistfully, "and it was an honour to work here."

"What happened to it?" Will asked, although he already knew the answer.

"He happened," Martha said raising an arm and pointing an accusing finger at the figure fast approaching them.

Will jumped back when he saw the figure that Martha was pointing at was Otto Crabtree himself.

"It's alright he can't see us, no one can. Here we are merely shadows. We can affect nothing, and nothing can affect us. If it was otherwise I would have long ago warned my younger self about what was going to happen."

"Then why are we here?" Will asked, his breathing slowing with the realisation that Otto was no threat here, "I mean if we can't touch or talk to anyone, what good is it that we are here?"

"We are not here to talk; we are here to watch."

There were so many questions that Will wanted to ask, but Martha's turned back told him in no uncertain terms that all questions would have to wait until she had shown him what she had brought him here to see.

So, without a word he followed her through the maze of corridors that was Crabtree Lodge.

Eventually, they came to a room on the upper level of the lodge that Will knew as a storeroom, but here it appeared to be someone's office. Will read the name on the door and turning to look at Martha he said, "Who's Dr Cutter?"

"Prepare yourself," was all that Martha said as she walked through the closed door.

"Oh," Will said as he watched the nurse vanish, "I can do that, no problem."

Taking a deep breath, he closed his eyes and stepped through the door after Martha.

When he opened his eyes on the other side, he found himself in a small, tidy office. There was a half-open window that looked out onto the well-kept grounds of the lodge, a filing cabinet to his left and an organised desk with a well-padded chair behind it just in front of him.

"I don't understand, Martha? What am I meant to see here?"

The only answer he received from the long-dead nurse was a raised finger to her lips in the universal gesture of silence and a slight nod to the closed office door.

As Will's eyes moved to the door, it opened and the living Martha of the past walked through it, followed by a man in a long white coat. At first, nothing registered with Will, but when he saw the doctor's face full-on; it was like looking into a mirror.

"That's me," he said, "I mean, it's really me."

"It is," said Martha in response, "but then again it's not."

"What the hell is going on, Martha?"

"Hear what they say and then I will try and answer all of your questions."

Will could see that he would get nothing more from the nurse at that moment so reluctantly he turned to watch the conversation that was about to unfold before him.

"Are you sure, Martha?" said Dr Cutter as he sat behind his desk, "please say you're not."

"I am, Jason," said the younger Martha sternly.

"But I examined Phillip myself. He died of natural causes. I know it's hard when someone so young dies like that but there were no suspicious circumstances. Phillip just died."

"No, he didn't, Jason. He was fine when I checked on him at ten yesterday, happy and talkative. But after Otto saw him that afternoon Phillip was in a terrible state; clammy, feverish and two hours later he was dead."

"But that doesn't mean that Otto killed him, Martha. All that means is that Phillip had a relapse and was too weak to recover."

"You know that's not true. Otto murdered that poor young boy. I don't know how and I don't know why. But he did and I'm sure of that."

"But where's your proof?" Cutter asked his voice matching her own for emotion.

"Proof, you know there's no proof. Otto is far too clever for that."

"Then what can I do?"

"You can confront him."

"And lose my job, is that what you want?"

"Your job, what does your job matter? I tell you, Jason if you don't do anything more of these children are going to die."

"Don't you think you're exaggerating a little? This is Otto Crabtree we're talking about."

"So, you're just going to sit there and do nothing, is that right?" Martha asked, leaning on the doctor's desk so that she could look him square in the eyes.

"There's nothing I can do. You have no proof and no witnesses. This is all just guesswork on your part."

"Alright, Jason, I'll go and see Otto myself and if anything happens to me then these children's deaths will be on your hands."

As Will watched the younger Martha leave the office he turned to his ghostly companion and said, "You sure had one hell of a temper."

"Yes, I did, but it did me very little good. You see, in two hours I will be found dead in the schoolroom."

"You're what? What happened?"

"They said it was a heart attack brought on by overwork. But it was Otto. The last thing I remember is him walking towards me across the schoolroom, and then whatever he did to poor Phillip he did to me."

"And him?" Will asked nodding his head towards the young doctor that looked so much like himself."

"Jason resigns tomorrow. I guess he was just too young and too afraid to face a monster like Otto."

"But why does he look so much like me?" Will said, still unable to take his eyes from the young doctor.

"He doesn't just look like you, he is you."

Before Will could ask another question Martha said, "It's like this Will. Jason does resign tomorrow, but what goes on here after he leaves haunts him for the rest of his life. He knew that Otto was murdering these children, but he just did not dare to face him, and that scarred him for the rest of his life. He died a young man full of remorse and opium."

"But if you were dead, how do you know how he died."

"Because, in part, I caused his death. My anger at Otto and my love for these children keep my soul here. It was I who found Cutter and to my everlasting shame I haunted him, telling him each time a child died."

"That's terrible," Will said, looking at the shade beside him in a new and quite different light.

"Yes, it was. Just one more thing I will have to answer for when my time comes to stand before God, but for the moment we are here to watch, so watch."

Almost as soon as Martha had finished speaking the door to Cutter's office opened and in walked Otto Crabtree. For a moment Otto stopped in the doorway and slowly looked around the room.

"Can he see us, Martha?"

The moment Will spoke Otto's head snapped around and looked directly at him. Will felt the blood freeze in his veins as he looked into the cold hard eyes of the hospital's administrator.

"Hello, doctor," Otto said as he pulled his eyes away from where Will was standing to look at Cutter, "I hear that Martha has been to see you again."

"But how do you know that? She's only just left here."

"Oh, you'd be surprised what I know," Otto said with a smile as he once again turned round to look at where Will was standing.

Cutter, seeing the way that Otto kept looking into the empty corner of his office, said, "What can I do for you, Otto?"

"You can disregard all that nonsense that Martha has been spouting of late, that's what you can do."

Will saw Cutter's whole body language change, "he's terrified of him," he thought as he watched the conversation continue in front of him.

"I'm not sure what you mean?" Cutter said, unable to look Otto in the eyes.

"I'm sure you do my dear boy. I just want you to remember who runs this hospital and who you rely on for your position here or any references that you might need in the future."

Will, who would have risen to such a threat, was shocked when Cutter simply said, "Yes Otto, whatever you say."

"Good. Well, seeing as we understand one another I'll bid you a good day."

Then just as he was about to leave the room Otto once more looked into the corner where Will and Martha were standing and said, "Sooner or later I will catch you, you know."

Once the office door had closed behind Otto, Will said, "I thought you said he couldn't see us, Martha."

"He can't, but Otto was and is still a very powerful spirit. In truth, he can't see us, but he can feel our presence."

Will didn't know what to say to this, so he turned to another question that had bothered him from the moment he had seen Cutter.

"Why do we look the same, Martha?"

Martha looked at the young man beside her for a long moment before she answered, "you have the same soul, it's why you can see us. Myself, the children, Otto. Poor Jason died with the deaths of Phillip and the others on his conscience and his unquiet spirit has wandered all this time, never resting, never at peace. Until it found in you a chance to redeem itself and avenge the innocents of this place."

At first, Will was shocked by what Martha had told him. But then, as if a curtain had been pulled back in his mind, Will realised that she was telling the truth.

"What do we do Martha? How do we stop him?"

"I don't know. I was never able to find out anything useful before he killed me. It was Jason who knew Otto's secrets."

"So now I do as well, is that what you're saying?"

"Yes, somehow you do even if you don't realise it yet. Otto's secrets are inside you, but for the moment that will have to wait. Our time here is over, and we must leave."

"How do we leave? I don't even know how we got here."

"Just close your eyes."

Will closed his eyes for only the slightest of moments before his alarm clock startled him to consciousness and he once more found himself in bed.

Chapter Eleven

Will wanted to dismiss what he'd witnessed as a simple dream because if it wasn't then the souls of the children that had died at Crabtree Lodge were his responsibility, and that was one that he didn't want. But deep down he knew that what he'd seen was what had happened. Somehow the soul of Jason Cutter had found its way back into the world to right the wrongs of the past. He was broken from these bleak and troubling thoughts by his phone.

"Hello?" Will said thickly, his voice full of sleep and emotion.

"Will?" asked Marie her voice full of concern, "you, OK?"

"Marie?"

"Surprised?"

"Well yes, seeing as how I didn't give you, my number."

"Well, there's no point having a key to the main office if you're not going to abuse it once in a while. You would be amazed at what I know about you now."

"And you're still talking to me?"

"I thought you might like to take me for breakfast before we go to work."

If Will could have seen Marie at that moment, he would have been very surprised. Over the phone, she sounded relaxed, confident. Almost blasé in fact, but the truth was very different indeed. She had tried to dial Will's number four times, each time hanging up before she had finished, and as she stood there waiting for his reply, which seemed to be taking an age, she couldn't help but think it had been a very bad idea.

"He's going to say no," she thought as she wound the phone's cord around her finger nervously, "I just know it."

"Yes OK, I'd like that. Where do you want to go?"

"Pick me up in an hour," she said, only just managing to keep the relief out of her voice, "I know this great little café in the centre of town."

"OK, see you in an hour."

As he showered Will once more thought about his dream; how strange and yet so very real it had seemed, and no matter how hard he tried to pass it off as just a simple nightmare he couldn't.

"Alright," he said aloud, as he plunged his head under the jet of hot steamy water, "it was real."

The moment he said this a strange kind of calm seemed to settle into his heart, like oil poured on to turbulent water, and just like that he knew what he had to do. He would stand against Otto Crabtree, he would save the children trapped in the lodge, and he would free Martha of the burden she had placed upon herself. Will had no idea how he was going to do these things, only that he was going to try.

As he dressed, he once again pored over his dream. Martha had said that he knew Otto Crabtree's secrets, that they were locked away inside of him. But how did you go about unlocking something for which you had no key?

"This is giving me a headache," he said, as he dressed in his cleanest jeans and t-shirt. "Maybe things will be clearer when I get to the lodge tonight."

Will took one more look at himself in the mirror, smiled at his reflection grabbed his car keys from the small table next to the front door and went to meet Marie for breakfast.

Twenty minutes later he pulled up outside Marie's building. He was just about to get out of his car when he saw her come out of the front door and walk down the small flight of stairs that led to the street.

"Hello," Marie said as she opened Will's passenger door and got in.

The subtle fragrance of Marie's perfume filled the small car, reminding Will of a summer's evening after a rain shower; cool, fresh and tantalising.

"Hello, so where are we going?"

"Head into town, if you park by the old town hall we can walk from there."

They drove in silence for a few minutes, each of them trying to think of a way to start a conversation. Then, as if on cue they both started talking at once.

"Go on, you first," smiled Marie.

"Are you still coming to my sister's birthday party tomorrow?"

"Yes, if I'm still invited that is?"

"You know you are. Anyway, if you don't go my sister will roast me, she's been dying to meet you."

"Been talking about me then, have you?"

"I have to talk about something, and you were a better subject than the weather."

"For that, you can buy breakfast."

Will pulled the car up to the kerb and they got out.

"The café's just up here," said Marie, slipping her arm through his.

The pair of them walked the few hundred metres to the café in companionable silence.

"You sure this is the right place?" Will said as they stopped outside the very small and unassuming café.

"Don't let the looks fool you. This is the best breakfast in town."

"Hello, Marie," said a large, ruby cheeked man as the pair of them walked through the door.

"Hi, Uncle Ken," Marie said smiling as she hugged the bear of a man who stood in front of her, "diet still going well I see."

"It would be, apart from all the food that Gill keeps cooking," said the big man with a smile, "anyway, take a table and I'll be right with you."

Will followed Marie to the rear of the café to a small table set next to the kitchen. As they sat down Will said, "So is this a family business?"

"My mum worked here when I was a kid. It's kind of where I grew up."

"Why do you always look at the menu, Marie?" said Ken as he walked up to the table. "You know you're going to order the same thing as every other time."

"I just like to look. Who knows, maybe one day I'll surprise you."

"Maybe," Ken said, taking a small order pad from the pocket of his shirt, "so what will it be?"

Marie studied the menu a moment longer, then putting it back onto the table she looked up at Ken and said, "I'll have two eggs, a sausage and a tomato please, Ken."

The big man smiled and turned his pad around so that Will could see that he had already written Marie's order on it.

"What did I say?" he said to Will, "over fifteen years I've known this girl and she's always had the same thing in my café."

Kate shrugged her shoulders and said, "I'm just a creature of habit."

"And what can I get for you Mr.?" Ken said, looking down at Will.

"You're the expert, Marie," Will said looking at her, "what would you recommend?"

"As this is your first time I would say try the Gill special. It's amazing."

"Alright then, I'll have the Gill special please."

"Now, Marie," Ken said laughing, "that's no way to treat your friend."

Will looked from Marie to Ken and back again,

"Alright, what's going on?"

"Sorry, Will," she said with a sly smile as she handed him the menu, "I couldn't resist it."

Will took the offered menu and felt his eyes widen as he read what was in the Gill special. "Three sausages," he said, reading the impressive list comprising the Gill special, "three rashers of bacon, three hash browns, fried tomatoes, mushrooms, beans, two eggs, chips, fried bread and toast."

"And it comes with free unlimited tea as well," Ken said once Will had finished.

"Does it come with a free defibrillator to start your heart once you've finished?" Will said putting the menu back on the table.

Ken and Marie burst out laughing.

"We're not sure," Ken said, "no one's finished it yet. Anyway, what can I get you?"

"Do you have something for an ordinary-sized man and not the jolly green giant?"

"Yes, we do," Ken said with pride, "and it's the best breakfast in town."

"Then I'll have that please."

Once Ken had gone to place their order Will said, "Your uncle seems a nice guy. Loud, but nice."

"Oh, he's not my real uncle," Marie said as she stood up to go and get them some knives and forks, "I just used to call him that when I was a kid and it stuck."

"And there was me thinking that you'd brought me here to meet your family."

Marie stopped, turned on her heel and looked Will square in the eyes. "Not yet dear, but when you do, you'll know it. They're a scary bunch."

"You can be a bit scary yourself, you know that don't you?"

"Good, isn't it?"

Will watched her walk to the front of the café to get their knives and forks and thought to himself,

"You've never met a girl like this before."

The breakfast was all that Marie had promised. Local sausages, eggs done to a turn, crispy bacon and freshly buttered toast all washed down with the biggest cup of tea that he had ever seen. The pair ate and talked, the walls of friendship breaking down, being subtly replaced by the newly budded bonds of romance without either of them noticing.

When the breakfast was finished Will pushed his plate away and said, "You were right, that was the best breakfast I've ever eaten."

"I told you Uncle Ken is the best."

Almost as if the mention of his name had summoned him from thin air Ken appeared at their table.

"Everything alright?" he asked, smiling, already knowing the answer.

"That was great," Will said, "can we have the bill please?"

"Bill?" said Ken looking surprised, "there's never a bill for my little strawberry."

"Oh my god, Ken," Marie said, her cheeks blushing a deep red with embarrassment.

"Strawberry?" Will asked unable to keep the smirk from his face.

"Yes alright," Marie said as her blush started to fade, "it was a childhood nickname. He's the only one who still calls me it. I'm sure you had one."

"Not me," said Will, still smiling at Marie's discomfort.

"Yes, well you can stop smiling now," Marie said as she got up, "you seem to be enjoying this just a little too much."

"Whatever you say, Strawberry."

Marie turned around quickly, her mock anger fading into laughter, "OK, I guess I would have done that as well, but now we had better get a move on or we're going to be late for work."

At the mention of Crabtree Lodge Will's dream came flooding back to him and suddenly the responsibility that he had taken upon himself seemed to weigh heavily on his shoulders.

"You, OK?" Marie said when she saw how serious he suddenly looked.

"Yes, I'm fine; just don't want to go to work."

"I know that feeling."

Will watched as she turned and walked out of the café.
"I bet you don't," he thought.

Chapter Twelve

The pair of them drove in companionable silence almost the whole way to the lodge.

"Look, Will," Marie said, as they pulled into the parking lot and parked next to her car, "would you mind if we kept our breakfast today to ourselves?"

Will looked at her for a moment before he answered, confusion flitting across his face.

"I guess so, but do you mind me asking why? It was only breakfast."

"I just like to keep my personal life personal. You've not worked here long, and this place is a hotbed of gossip. Everyone wants to know everyone else's business, and I don't want us to become just another topic in the staff room."

"You want to keep me a secret so that you can have me all to yourself, is that right?"

"Down boy, I just like to keep things to myself. What do you say?"

"Yes, OK, whatever makes you happy."

"Keep talking like that and we are going to get on very well."

Will smiled as all manner of thoughts flashed across his mind. He got out of the car and walked with Marie to the lodge entrance.

"I'll see you at tea break," she said as they walked in through the main doors, "I've got to go and write my report about Joan."

"Alright, see you then."

The moment Marie vanished into the office Will walked over to the picture that dominated the hallway. He was curious to see what if anything had changed. He couldn't help but smile when he saw that the young boy at the front was smiling at him and the little girl who he now knew as Margery no longer had such a crestfallen look on her young face.

"Hello, Margery," he said quietly and blew the little girl a kiss before he walked off to the staff room to get ready for his shift.

He didn't notice the shadows below the picture gather, and for a moment they seemed to watch him before falling back.

The first part of the shift flew past, and before he knew it, he was back in the staff room drinking tea and laughing with his colleagues.

"Did you get Marie home alright yesterday?" Sally asked as she handed him a cup of tea.

"I bet he did," said John, loudly and full of innuendo before Will could answer.

The laughter that broke out in the room died just as swiftly as Will turned to face the older man. He was just about to tell John to keep his mouth shut when Marie's words from earlier came back to him. If he jumped at the other man's barb then the whole team would know that something was going on, so instead, he handed John his tea, winked and said, "I could tell you, but I wouldn't want that old ticker of yours to be pushed too hard."

John stood there for a moment, then his face split into a huge grin. "As if Marie would be seen with you anyway," he said laughing.

"As if Marie would be seen with whom?" said Marie as she walked into the staff room for her break.

"I was just joking with Will, Marie, that's all," John said, a little red coming to his cheeks.

"And what were you joking about?" Marie asked, her voice just a shade too soft for John's comfort.

"He wanted to know if you and I got together when I took you home yesterday," Will said, smiling at John's discomfort.

Marie laughed, a genuine, good-natured sound, and pinching the older man hard on the bum she said, "What, and cheat on you, John?"

"Alright," Sally said, laughing just as much as the rest of her staff. "I think that's enough before John here goes so red we can use him as a heat lamp."

The staff room broke into more laughter and then people drifted into their own conversations about their days off or holidays coming up. Everything apart from Will and Marie and if they were or were not involved with each other. As Marie walked past Will to pick up an empty cup, she gave him the quickest of winks.

As he suppressed his smile he thought, "I think I'm going to enjoy this secret romance thing."

All too soon for Will the tea break was over, and he was once again on his own in the silent, deserted corridors of the lodge, although he now knew that these seemingly empty corridors were populated by Otto Crabtree's young, innocent victims.

It was as he was cleaning the old schoolroom that he had his first encounter of the night with the children of the lodge.

"Hello, Will," said a small voice from behind him as he swept the old school's floor.

Will jumped despite himself and whipped round to see the small, fragile form of Margery smiling up at him.

"Hello," Will said, kneeling so that he could look the little girl in the eyes, "what can I do for you?"

"Nothing, I wanted to say hello, that's all."

Will, sensing that this was not all, stayed silent and waited for the little girl to continue.

"I just wanted to say thank you," Margery said, her voice even smaller than before.

"Thank you? What for?"

"For saying that you would help us. I never thought that anyone would."

Will felt humbled by the confidence that he heard in Margery's voice. It spoke of pain and terror and hope unrealised but never abandoned. He smiled at her, and trying to lighten the sombre mood that had suddenly settled around them he said, "Where are the others, Margery?"

"I'm not allowed to say," she answered nervously.

"It's alright if you're not allowed to say, that's fine."

"You mean you won't hurt me for not telling?"

"Of course not, why would I?"

"Because you're a grown-up just like Otto, and he hurts me."

Will could almost feel his heartbreak when he heard Margery say this. Otto had not only imprisoned the children's spirits in this hateful place, but he also held their emotions hostage. To them, grown-ups were creatures to be feared. Only Martha held their trust, and she had bought that with her life and soul.

"I'm not Otto, you don't have to tell me anything, and I won't hurt you, I promise."

Margery smiled for a moment, then she turned and ran into the shadows behind him, leaving him alone.

"Was it something I said?" Will asked the empty room.

About half an hour later, just as Will was going to leave the schoolroom, Margery stepped out of the shadows beside him and said, "Would you like to meet the others?"

"But I thought you said."

"I asked Martha, she said it was alright."

"In that case, I would love to."

"Take my hand," Margery said, holding out her hand with a smile of her own.

Will hesitated for a moment unsure if he would be able to hold the little girl's hand.

"It's alright, just trust me."

Will didn't answer, he just reached for her hand. He could see her hand in his but all he could feel was a warm caress as if someone had breathed gently on his skin.

"Don't let go, Will," Margery said as she started to walk towards the shadows that sat in the corner of the room.

"What happens if I do, Margery?" he asked and was immediately sorry he had when he saw the look that crossed the young girl's face.

"Just don't," was all she said in answer.

"Alright," Will said under his breath as the two of them stepped into the darkness.

Will's vision blurred and a sudden chill ran the length of his body. He sensed that the emptiness that surrounded him was more than infinite and on the most primeval level Will knew that if he did lose his grip on Margery's hand then he would wander lost and alone here until the stars went cold and the universe itself grew old and died. He felt like he was in this terrible place for an age but his time there was no more than the distance between one moment and the next.

"Hello," Martha said softly, as he found himself on solid ground once more, in a small, bare, dimly lit room. He was never more pleased to see someone than he was the long-dead nurse.

"What was that?" he asked as he let go of the little girl's hand.

"We call it the in-between. It's what fills all the empty places of existence."

"What? That makes no sense at all."

"It does for us. The in-between fills the space between thoughts and the gaps between words. It fills up empty holes and daydreams. It is everything else that is not something."

"Well, that's clearer, thanks for explaining that to me."

"I'm sorry Will, it's not meant to be a place for the living to know about or to see. We understand it because we are a part of it and it of us."

"Well, one thing I do understand is that it's not a place I want to see again anytime soon."

"I don't blame you. Even we can become lost there, and if that happens it happens forever."

For a moment Will was lost for words as the image of being trapped in the in-between again raced across his imagination.

"Where are the other children, Martha?" he asked, trying to rid the thoughts from his mind.

As soon as Will mentioned the children Martha's expression darkened.

"I think Otto has one of them," she said.

"What? What will he do?"

"You know, you heard Bruno's story. He steals their energy. He rips it from them, and the worst thing is that he will do it repeatedly. It might be a day, a month, a year or even a decade, but he will do it again. There is never an end for them."

As she finished speaking the shadows to Will's left shimmered and the rest of the children stepped into the room.

"It was George, Martha," Phillip said, walking up to the nurse.

"Where is he, Phillip?" Martha asked as she searched the small group of children.

The ghost of Otto's first and most favourite victim lowered his head and spoke softly, "he's gone. Otto drained him completely."

"But why? Why would he discard one of you like that? He needs you all to survive. Otto is evil and cruel, not stupid."

"He was laughing as he did it, Martha," Phillip said, his eyes filling with tears, "laughing. He said he didn't need someone as weak as George anymore. He said that soon he would have another soul to feed upon, a new soul."

"But how? He can only feed on children and children don't come here anymore."

"What's going on, Martha?" Will asked, "is George dead now? I mean really dead?"

It was Phillip who answered Will's question, his voice full of anger and loss.

"Yes, Will, really dead. We've lost our friend."

"I'm sorry, Phillip," Will said, "I wish there was something I could do."

"I don't want to sound hard or harsh," Martha said, breaking into their exchange, "but George is gone and there is nothing we can do for him. But Otto has designs on another child and we cannot let that happen."

Chapter Thirteen

It was Phillip who took Will back through the in-between to the schoolroom. Once more he felt the bone-chilling loneliness of that terrible place and silently promised himself that if he could he would avoid going there again at all costs.

"I'm truly sorry about George, Phillip," he said when they were back in the welcome and very ordinary old schoolroom.

"So am I," Phillip said sadly, "he was my best friend and even though he will never have to endure Otto's attention again, part of me wishes he was still here."

"And that makes you feel bad?"

"Yes, it does, what does that make me? When I would rather have my friend here suffering than for him to be gone and finally at rest."

"It just means you're human, that's all. You miss your friend, what's more, human than that?"

The young boy smiled at this, and Will could see a weight of guilt raise from his shoulders.

"Thanks," Phillip said.

"What do you think Otto meant?" Will asked.

"You mean about a new soul? I don't know. As Martha said, Otto can only feed on children and children simply don't come here anymore."

"But what would happen if one did?"

"Nothing good. For a living child, Otto can seem to be a kind of fantasy. They see him as a smiling, good-natured ghost. He whispers to them, telling them secrets that he knows will entice them into coming here alone."

"Secrets?"

"Things that grownups just wouldn't understand. He tells them about magical lands and wonderful secret treasures, everything they want to hear."

"Is that what he did to you?"

"Yes, it was while I was ill. He came to me, and he showed me the most amazing things. The more he showed me the more I wanted him to show me. He told me that when I died, I would live in these places, but all I did was stay here and watch as he did the same thing to so many other children."

Will opened his mouth to speak but was stopped by Phillip's suddenly up-raised hand.

"Someone's coming," he whispered.

Before Will could ask who it was, the young boy vanished, just as the door to the schoolroom opened and Marie walked in, a smile on her face.

"Well don't look so happy to see me," she said, her smile dropping a little when she saw the serious look on Will's face.

"Oh, sorry, I've got a bit of a headache coming on."

"Massage is always a good cure for that."

"Now there's an offer," Will said, as Marie moved behind him and started rubbing his head.

"If you're nice to me at your sister's party tomorrow, maybe you'll get a better one."

"Party?"

"You're sister's birthday party? The one you invited me to last week, remember? You do still want to take me, don't you?" Marie said, a very subtle tremor leaking into her voice.

"What, God, yes of course I do,

"Are you sure, Will? Because if you don't then I would rather know now than look a fool later."

"Marie, please. I do want you to go and I want you to meet her and her family, they're the best. Especially little Jason, he's great. You're going to love him."

At the mention of his nephew's name, Will felt certain that the temperature in the room dropped a degree or two. He shuddered.

"Someone walk over your grave?" Marie asked.

"What makes you say that?"

"Nothing really, it's just an expression."

"I'm sorry, it's just been one of those nights."

"That's OK, I forgive you. But only if you're extra nice to me tomorrow."

"Of course I will be."

"In that case, I'll leave you to get on with your work. Oh, and make sure you get some sleep during the day. Who knows, you might need it."

Before he could ask what, she meant Marie was gone and he was alone again.

"What do you make of that?" he said to the empty room.

"I think she likes you," Phillip said as he stepped out of the shadows.

"No one likes an eavesdropper, Phillip."

"I'm sorry I didn't mean to listen to your private conversation, but Martha thought you should know."

"Know what?"

"It's possible that Marie is the one helping Otto."

"That's ridiculous."

"Just because you like her doesn't mean that you know everything about her."

"Well, no, of course not, but still."

"We're not saying she is his accomplice. What we're saying is be careful of what you tell her. We trust you Will, not your girlfriend."

Will was just about to protest again but the look on Phillip's face stopped him.

"OK you're right, I'll watch what I say, and I won't tell her anything about you or the others."

"Thank you."

"But why do you suspect her?"

"Marie has been working here at the lodge for a long time, and she has never been scared or runoff, not even when she has been in the room on her own. That makes us suspicious."

"Which room?"

"Up on the second floor at the far end of the corridor. It's kept locked now and never used because every patient that has ever been in there has died in only a few days. It was once Otto's office and it's now where he goes when he has drained one of us. He lurks in there like a snake after a meal, sated and bloated on our energy and life."

Will realised that the room Phillip was talking about must be the same room that Bruno had fallen asleep in. Before he could say this the shadows beside him shimmered and Margery appeared beside him.

"Martha says it's time to come back, Phillip," she said, her voice as quiet and singsong as always.

"Alright," Phillip said smiling at the little girl as he held out his hand to her, "let's go."

Will watched as the children walked into the shadows and vanished. A moment later Phillip's voice drifted back.

"Remember, tell her nothing and whatever you do, if you go into that room, do not fall asleep."

Will picked up his broom and started sweeping, trying his hardest to lose himself in his work for the rest of the shift.

He was glad when the hands of the large hall clock ticked their way to eight o'clock. He packed away his cleaning equipment and made his way to the staff room to get his things.

When he got there the room was a hive of activity with the night shift going off and the day shift coming on. He chatted with a few of the staff, laughed with others. But this was mostly done on autopilot as his mind was almost completely occupied with the night's events. It was only once he had walked out of the large entrance doors of the lodge and into the new day's sun that he breathed a sigh of relief and felt truly safe.

"That's a big sigh."

Will turned and looked down into the smiling face of his new girlfriend as she sat in her car.

"Just been a long night I guess."

"Then you'd best get some sleep before you pick me up tonight because I don't want you falling asleep on me."

"Don't worry about that, I'll make sure I'm bright-eyed and bushy tailed."

"Pick me up at seven and we can have a drink before we go to your sister's place if you like?"

Before he had a chance to say that he did like, Marie pulled away and out of the parking lot.

"She never gives me a chance to answer."

As he drove home Will thought about what had happened the night before. There always seemed to be more questions than answers, and even when he did seem to get an answer often it led to even more questions. Like whom was the child coming to the lodge? How were they going to get there? What exactly was the in-between? Who was helping Otto and why? He had all the questions but none of the answers.

It was with another sigh that he opened his front door and walked into his flat. One thing he liked about living alone was having no one to answer to. If he didn't want to talk to anyone he didn't have to. There was no forced conversation after a hard day, no trying to make that other person feel like he was happy to see them when all he wanted was a shower and to climb into bed.

But now as he undressed and stepped under the hot water, he found that all he could think about was Marie; how she sounded, how she looked when she smiled, how that smile lit up the room. No matter how much he tried to push her from his mind she always fought her way back in. He put some coffee on and there she was. He put on a CD, and she was there listening to it with him. She seemed to be everywhere he turned and to his surprise, he found that he liked it.

But then what Phillip had said came back to him; that they didn't trust her, that she could be the one helping Otto.

"Please don't let it be her," Will said aloud, "anyone but her."

He knew there was no guarantee it wasn't her. If it was and he asked her she would lie, and if it wasn't and he asked her she would think that he was insane. Either way was out of the question. The only thing he could do was what Philip had suggested: keep it all to himself and tell Marie nothing.

It was with these thoughts and a hundred more running around inside his head that Will finally fell into bed and thankfully into a dreamless sleep.

Chapter Fourteen

When Will woke up later that day he felt completely disoriented. His sleep had been so deep that for a moment he could not work out where he was. Nothing that his eyes lighted on seemed familiar, but as the seconds passed and the fog of sleep lifted from his mind, he realised he was in bed at home, and safe after the night he had spent at Crabtree Lodge. He let his body relax, and the duvet and pillows seemed to wrap themselves around him of their own volition as he felt himself drift softly back to sleep.

As his eyes started to close, he caught sight of his alarm clock. At first, nothing registered as wrong until suddenly he realised what the small clock was telling him: it was five-thirty, he'd forgotten to set the alarm.

If there had been an Olympic sport for showering and shaving in the shortest time then Will would have been guaranteed the silver, with a good chance of the gold. He ran to his car, his shirt flapping as he tried to button it. The drive to Marie's was more like a rally cross event than a journey through the centre of town. He pulled to a screeching stop outside her flat just as the small clock on his dashboard flashed onto eighteen fifty-nine.

"Not bad," he said to himself as he got out of the car.

He took a moment to smooth his dark blue shirt, take the bottom of his black trousers out of the top of his socks, and check his shoes to indulge his paranoia, making sure that he was wearing some and not, as he had worried for the briefest moment, a slipper and a trainer. Finally satisfied that he looked ok, he climbed the steps to the main door and taking a deep breath, pushed gently on her doorbell.

"Hello?" said Marie, her voice muffled and metallic as it passed through the small intercom speaker.

"It's Will."

"Oh hello, come up I won't be long. I'm flat three"

When he heard the buzz of the door lock disengaging, he pushed open the ornate door and made his way to Marie's flat.

"Hello," he said, as he pushed open the already half-opened door,

"There's wine on the table, help yourself. Pour me one as well, will you?"

Before he could answer Marie had disappeared back into her bedroom and the unmistakable sound of a hairdryer drifted into the living room.

"So, there was no need to rush then," Will said quietly as he poured wine into the two waiting glasses.

It was twenty minutes later when Marie at last emerged. When he heard the door open Will was at first going to say something sarcastic about her not having a clock, but as soon as he saw her any comment like that was driven from his mind to be replaced by only one word.

"Wow."

Gone was the strict, uniform-clad assistant head nurse. In her place stood someone that he had never seen. Marie's normally tightly tied hair fell about her shoulders in a long, elegant wave. Her uniform had been replaced by a beautiful, black, short-sleeved top that had a plunging neckline, showing off Kate's breasts to perfection. Her long, well-formed legs were accentuated by a tight-fitting black skirt that reached to just above her knees and a pair of shiny black high-heeled sling backs. The whole transformation was topped off by a small and so far, undisclosed butterfly tattoo that stood out gracefully from Marie's left ankle.

"Will I do?" she said as she did a complete turn for Will.

"Err yes."

"Good, because I didn't have a thing to wear."

"Well for someone with nothing to wear you've done alright."

"Now you're just being nice."

Marie didn't go out much and apart from her job she didn't really socialise, just the occasional drinks with friends or a meal with her family. She had tried her best to look good for Will and it felt good for her efforts to be appreciated in such a forthright way.

"We'd better be going; my sister will kill me if we're late."

"Hang on just a moment," Marie said as she handed him her wine glass and hurried back into her bedroom. She appeared a moment later carrying a small ornate bag and a pink envelope.

"What's that?"

"I can't go to your sister's birthday without a present, can I?" she answered as she picked up a small silver wrap from the back of her couch and spread it across her shoulders.

"You didn't have to get her anything."

"Of course I did. Anyway, it's only something small."

Once they were in the car Marie said, "do you mind if tonight we don't talk about work?"

"If that's what you want, why?"

"It's just what with everything that's been happing there lately it would be nice to forget the place even if it's just for one night."

"That works for me."

As they drove the pair's conversation meandered from one topic to another. They talked about Will's sister and her family, about the latest films, and about the forthcoming solar eclipse.

"I still can't believe you hadn't heard about that," Marie said.

"Why? I bet there must be hundreds of people who haven't heard about it."

"Only if they've been living under a rock for the past six months, the damn thing's been all over the news and in every newspaper for ages."

"Then I guess I must just be stupid."

"Yes, I was thinking it must be something like that."

They got out of the car laughing to be greeted by the sounds of a party in full swing. Before they could knock on the front door it was opened by Max, her face flushed and happy with tomorrow's hangover already baking in her head.

"BB," she said loudly as she gave him a sloppy kiss and a half-drunken hug.

"Hi, Sis, this is Marie, remember me telling you about her?"

The change in Will's sister was almost immediate. Gone was the slightly drunken young woman and in her place stood Will's older sister, who immediately started to scrutinise Marie from head to foot in the same way that women have done to each other since time began.

"Hi, I'm Max."

"Hi, Max, I've brought you a little something, I hope you like it."

Max took the small bag and card and said, "thank you, Marie, it's so nice of you. At least you remembered, unlike other people."

"You didn't get your sister a present?" Marie said as she stepped into the house.

"Of course I did, I've just left it in the boot is all. I'll be right back; Will dashed back to his car leaving the two women alone.

"What an airhead," Max said as she watched him disappear.

"Yes, but he's got a nice bum," Marie said without thinking.

Max looked at her for a moment, smiled and said, "come on, I'll introduce you to everyone."

Marie had a great time at the party, dancing and laughing with Max as they realised that each had found a natural friend.

"She seems nice, Will," said Brian as he walked up to his brother-in-law and offered him a beer.

"No thanks, Brian, I've got my car, and I've already had a glass of wine at Marie's."

"Have a drink, Will," Marie said as she and Max came up to the men, "we can always get a cab."

"Yes, you have to have a drink at your sister's party BB," Max said as she put her arm around her husband.

"That's the second time you've called him BB, Max, what does it mean?"

"Don't you dare, Maxine," Will said pointing a warning finger at his sister.

"Oh dear," Max said, flashing a smile as she dragged her husband away, "come on stud, dance with me."

"So, where's this adorable nephew you were telling me about?" Marie asked, thinking that Will needed plying with a few more drinks to loosen his tongue.

"He's staying at his Nan's for the night. Max and Brian thought it might be too noisy for him here tonight."

"Yes, they might have a point," Marie said with a smile.

"But trust me you are going to like him, everyone does."

"You plan on there being another date then?"

Will side-stepped her comment as best he could by saying, "do you want another drink?"

"Only if you have one as well."

"I can't, I had that glass at yours and if I have any more and get pulled over that's my license."

"Have a drink, we can get a cab. Tomorrow, I'll pick you up for work and we can come here and get your car at the end of the shift, what do you say?"

"I say that that is the best plan I've heard in ages."

"So, what's it to be?" Marie said as she looked at the huge array of drink that stood in front of her.

"You're idea, your choice."

"In that case, we'll start with tequila slammers and move on from there."

The pair of them were just about to take on their third slammer when Max and Brian appeared beside them.

"You decided to have a drink after all," Brian said putting one massive arm around his brother-in-law's shoulders and hugging him, "good man."

"Put him down, Brian," Max said when she saw how crushed Will looked inside her husband's arm, "before you break him."

"Sorry," Brian said, "so what are you drinking?"

"Tequila slammers," Marie said, answering for Will as she suddenly knocked back her glass, "and he's one behind now."

"Come on, Will," Brian said picking up Will's glass in one huge hand and offering it to him, "you can't be beaten by a girl."

"That," Max said walking away from her husband to stand beside Marie, "sounds like a challenge."

"What do you say, Will?" Brian asked laughing, "Do you think we can take them?"

"Totally."

"Right then," Max said as she poured out four glasses of tequila, the rules, the first one who can't drink their drink or passes out loses for their team."

"And what do the winner's get?" Brian asked as he picked up his drink.

"The losers," Max said with a very mischievous smile as she sank her first glass.

Each team sank their shots of tequila one after another and very soon a small crowd had gathered around them, the women cheering on Max and Marie and the men doing the same for Brian and Will.

"You're looking a little pale, lover," Max said as she watched Brian pick up his next full glass, "you sure you can manage it?"

"Don't worry about me, babe," Brian said as he threw the golden liquid quickly down his throat. But despite his boast, Brian did look the worse for wear as his sixth tequila hit his system.

"Your turn," Max said as she handed her teammate a glass.

Marie took the glass and looked at Will for a moment, winked, then downed its contents in a single swallow. The women in the room erupted in applause in response to this bravado. Marie then picked up a filled glass from the bar and passed it to Will, saying, "your turn, BB."

He took the offered glass and turning round with the glass held high he said, "This is just too easy," and sank the shot in one go.

Then it was Max again. She picked up her glass and without a flourish or a word swallowed it in one, grabbed another glass and handed it to her husband.

Brian looked at it for a moment his face a few shades paler than it was the previous round.

"You ok, baby?" Max said a huge smile on her face.

"I'm fine."

He held the glass a moment longer then taking a deep breath he lifted the glass to his lips and emptied its contents into his mouth.

The room went silent as everyone watched Brian. He held the tequila in his mouth for a moment, then quite suddenly turned his back on the crowd and spat it back into the glass.

The women in the room erupted in victory. Max and Marie hugged each other and screamed. Will turned to make sure that his bother-in-law was alright but was surprised to find Brian with a huge smile on his face and showing no ill effects from the competition at all.

"What's going on?" Will asked.

"Trust me, that was one game that being the loser makes you the winner," Brian answered with a wink as Max appeared beside them.

"You're my slave now, husband."

"Whatever you say, mistress."

The light that had failed to go on in Will's mind finally became a blazing beacon. Max and Marie may have been annoyed that they had lost and reluctant to play the role of slaves, but to lose meant that not only were they now in the best of moods but they could claim both men as prizes, and that could only be for the good.

"You're a clever man, Brian," Will thought as he saw Marie walking towards him.

"You now belong to me," she said.

"I guess so."

"Good, go and get me a drink and I will try and decide what to do with my prize."

As he collected drinks for them both Will couldn't help but imagine what Marie might have planned for him now that she had won.

As he was about to walk away from the bar a huge arm curled around his shoulders and a voice said, "say thank you, Brian,"

Will turned round to look into the smiling face of his brother-in-law.

"Thank you, Brian."

"Now you go and have a good time because I have to make sure that your sister gets everything she asks for."

"Too much information," Will laughed, as Brian walked back to his wife.

When he got back to Marie Will handed her a drink and said, "Is there anything else I can do for you?"

"Yes, there is. You can call us a cab because I've thought of a few things that I want you to do."

"Yes, my lady. Just let me say goodbye to Max."

"OK, but don't take too long, slave."

As he looked for his sister Will called a cab with his mobile. He found Max and Brian in the kitchen lost in a deep kiss.

"We're off now Max."

"Ok BB, say goodbye to Marie for me. I like her."

Will kissed his more than a little drunk sister on the cheek, and with a final wave, he went back to Marie and together they walked outside to wait for the taxi.

So late at night, the journey back to Marie's flat was much quicker. Once they were back inside Marie threw her wrap carelessly on the couch.

"There's wine in the kitchen, slave," she said commandingly, "go fetch me some."

Will couldn't help but smile as he went into the kitchen to look for the wine. Brian could not have been more right, losing that contest had been the only way to win. He found the wine and a couple of glasses and took them back into the front room where Marie was standing by the window looking out into the night.

"Wine my lady."

Marie smiled and walked over to him.

"So why BB?"

Will put the glasses down on the low coffee table and poured the wine.

"It's a childhood nickname. When I was born, I was covered in this soft blonde hair. When Max saw me, she called me Blonde Bill. It stuck and eventually got shortened to BB."

"You were blonde all over?"

"Yes, just about."

Marie put down her glass and put her arms around his neck and said huskily, "show me."

Chapter Fifteen

Will woke in the early hours of the morning with Marie wrapped luxuriously around him. He smiled at her sleeping face as their night together passed across his mind's eye. With the images came arousal and Will considered waking her for a repeat performance, but then the reason that he had woken up drifted back to him and his lust faded as quickly as it had risen. He knew that something at the lodge was wrong. He didn't know what, but he knew it was something bad.

As he lay there trying to decide what to do, the bedside phone rang. The sudden noise amid all the quiet made him jump. His movement combined with the harsh tones woke Marie from her sleep. She grabbed for the phone and in a sleep-filled voice said, "hello?"

The sleep vanished in a heartbeat as whatever was said to her brought her to a concerned and startled wakefulness.

"Alright, Sally I'll be there right away."

"What's wrong?"

"I don't know, there's been some kind of incident, but she wouldn't say any more as she has to call the rest of the nurses."

"But you can't drive; you must be well over the limit still with all that tequila you've had."

Marie paused for a moment, her sweatshirt half on and half off.

"Damn I forgot about that. I don't suppose?"

"Don't even think about asking me, I've had just as much to drink as you."

"Yes, I guess you're right. Alright, can you call me a taxi while I finish getting dressed?"

By the time Will had made the call, Marie was dressed and desperately trying to drink as much water and eat as many biscuits as she could to get her head straight and re-hydrate herself.

"Do you want me to come with you?"

"No, if we turn up together everyone will know that you were here and I would like to keep you a secret for a while yet. Things will be more fun that way, you don't mind, do you?"

"Not if there are more nights like last night I don't."

"Oh yes, like that and better. I've got some fantastic ideas for you Blonde Bill."

As they stood there holding each other and kissing there was the unmistakable sound of a car pulling up outside.

"That must be my taxi," Marie said as she pushed herself gently away.

"Can you drop me at my place? You go right past it on the way."

"Only if you jump out quickly because whatever is going on must be serious for Sally to be calling in all the off-duty staff."

"Just open the door and throw me out."

Ten minutes later the taxi pulled up outside Will's flat.

"Call me when you can and let me know what's going on," he said and kissed her before climbing out of the taxi.

"If I can," she said as the door closed and the taxi pulled away, disappearing into the traffic.

He walked into his flat lost in thought; what had happened at the lodge to make Sally call in the off-duty staff? Whatever it was it must be serious.

"Well, nothing I can do about it from here," he said to the empty flat.

With a helpless shrug, he decided that the best thing he could do was get some rest, but as he undressed Will realised that he was not in the least bit tired, and he knew that if he went to bed that all he would do would be to lay there staring at the ceiling.

While he tried to decide what to do, he went and had a shower. The hot water felt good on his skin, washing the night's experiences from his body. Once he'd finished, he put on a pot of coffee to percolate then went and turned on his games system. Picking up the control pad he said, "Alright, time to kill some zombies."

The time flew past, and the early hours passed into dawn and then full morning before he had even realised. It was only the ringing of his phone that brought him out of the virtual world in which he had lost himself.

He pressed the pause button on his game and picked up the phone handset.

"Hello?"

"Will, it's me," said Marie, her voice sounding tired and haggard.

"Marie, how are you? What happened at the lodge?"

"I can't talk for long, it's still so busy here."

"What happened?"

"The patients have had the worst night I can remember, all of them. It's like a madhouse, we've got people running around naked, some of them dancing in the gardens, even one woman who has locked herself in one of the supply cabinets and is refusing to come out until we get rid of the monster, whatever that means."

"I know what it means," thought Will, but what he said was, "do you want me to come in? Is there anything I can do?"

Will could hear the sigh of gratitude in his new girlfriend's voice at his offer and was touched by it.

"If you could that would be great, we need everyone we can get to clean this place up and I could do with the support."

"Alright, I'll be there just as soon as I can."

He hung up the phone, called a cab and made himself some toast. By the time he had eaten and dressed and gone outside, he only had a few moments to wait before the taxi pulled up.

"Crabtree Lodge please," he said as he jumped into the back seat of the car.

Without a word, the taxi driver did a quick turn in the middle of the road and headed off in the direction of the lodge.

Fifteen minutes later Will was paying the taxi fare and looking at his workplace in amazement. Every door and window was open and the noise that was coming from inside reminded him more of a Victorian insane asylum than the modern nursing home that it was.

As he walked quickly to the door one of the patients, a man he didn't know, ran past him waving a large tablecloth, almost as if he was trying to scare something away. The man was quickly pursued by John and one of the nursing staff.

"Having fun, John?" Will said unable to resist teasing his friend.

"Wait till you get inside laughing boy, there's more than enough work for you and your bucket."

Will left the two of them to try and calm the agitated man down and walked into the lodge.

John had not been exaggerating. The place was a mess. There was rubbish and up-turned furniture everywhere. Will had only gotten halfway to the staff room when he bumped into Sally. The normally calm and quiet head nurse looked just how Marie had sounded.

"Hi, Sally, I came to help," he said, "what can I do?"

"Hi, Will, and thanks. We have a blocked sink that's half-flooded one of the upstairs bathrooms, every table and chair in the canteen is somehow out in the gardens, and it looks like every patient has decided to wreck their rooms. So, take your pick."

"And what do you want me to do after tea break?"

Sally looked at him for a second, then her face changed and she laughed.

"Thanks, I needed that, start with the flooded bathroom please."

Will went to the staff room, grabbed his stuff and made his way up to the first floor. What he found was if anything even more of a mess than the ground floor. Each of the patients' doors was ajar with furniture and bed linen everywhere.

"Wow," he said to himself, "some party."

For the best part of the next two hours, Will set about cleaning the place up. He picked up all the linen and brought the nurses and auxiliaries clean bedclothes from the laundry. He managed to get the sink in the flooded bathroom unblocked and was just in the process of mopping up the last of the water when he heard a welcome voice say.

"Not exactly what I was hoping to do this morning."

Will turned and looked at Marie and said, "no, me neither. How are you doing?"

"I've been better; I just don't understand what happened here. The whole place has just erupted. I tell you we're lucky that no one's been hurt. As it is we're going to have to get agency people in for a day or two as there's no way that the normal staff can cope. Most have been here since last night and I think we're all just about done in."

"Well, every cloud, Marie."

"What on earth are you talking about?" she said getting a little angry that he would suggest anything good could come out of the chaos around them.

"Only that if we don't have to work tonight maybe I could come round to your place, and we could relax each other."

"You know what, I think that might just be what I need after all this."

They parted with a smile and went about their respective jobs.

A short while later Will was in the old schoolroom cleaning the walls and floor of the mud that one of the patients had managed to drag into the room through the back door. Out of the corner of his eye, he saw the now-familiar shimmering shadows that heralded the arrival of Martha or one of the children. He stopped washing the walls and stared, waiting to see who it was. After a moment Phillip stepped out of the shadows.

"What happened here, Phillip?"

"It was Otto," said the young boy, as he jumped onto a box and sat down, "this is something he does. He gets bored and this is his way of having fun. The first time he did it was twenty years after I died. Two patients died and one of the staff was found hanged in the morgue. The last time was fifty years ago. No one died then but two of the staff resigned that day and one of the patients went insane. All in all, this time has been quite tame."

"But why do this?"

"Why not? The man is evil, truly evil. He revels in the pain and misery of others and delights in mayhem and destruction."

"All this was just for fun?"

Phillip didn't answer he just nodded his head.

Changing the subject, Will said, "Have you found out who's helping him yet?"

"Not yet. We know that it's one of the staff but each time Otto meets with them he shrouds himself so that we can't see."

"Shrouds himself?"

"Otto is a very powerful spirit. The mayhem he's caused here is only a small showing of that power."

"So how on earth do we fight something like him?"

"The same way we have for over a hundred years," Phillip said as he jumped down from his box seat, "with our hearts and our faith and our friendship."

Will felt a little humbled by the dignity in Phillip's words and it suddenly struck him that despite how he looked Phillip was, in fact, a warrior. One who had been at war for over a hundred and twenty years, a war that took no prisoners and had no rules. Yet it had not corrupted the boy's spirit but rather had ennobled it.

"I have to go now," Phillip said as he walked back towards the shadows, "I only came to tell you that Otto will be asleep for the next few days. All this pain and anguish is like a banquet for him, and he has stuffed himself."

"That's one thing at least."

"Yes, it is, but remember his accomplice is still here, so please watch yourself. If we know about them then there is every chance that they know about you."

Will watched Phillip disappear into the darkness.

"That's a comforting thought," he said to the now empty room.

Chapter Sixteen

Eventually, Crabtree Lodge was clean and tidy and as operational as it could be. All those who had worked so hard to restore the lodge to its former state were gathered in the staff room enjoying a well-earned tea break and waiting for Sally to come and talk to them.

"How are you doing?" Will asked as he walked up to Marie.

"Apart from feeling like I've been dragged through a hedge backwards and in desperate need of a shower I'm fine."

"Well, that was fun," said John, interrupting the young couple.

"that's your idea of fun is it, John?" Marie asked him sarcastically, "remind me never to come to a party at your place."

"Trust me," John said, a wicked smile on his face, "if you came to my place Marie you'd have the time of your life."

"I couldn't do that to you John, not a man in your condition."

The people nearest the threesome laughed and one of them said, "John when are you ever going to learn that you're never going to get the better of her?"

"I live in hope," said the older man with a smile, "does anyone want another cup?"

His offer was met with a unanimous yes, so John went about the mammoth task of making the whole room another round of drinks. As he was doing this the staff room door opened and Sally walked in looking just as tired as everyone else.

"Can I have your attention please people?" she said, clapping her hands together.

The room went silent, and everyone stopped to look at her.

"Alright, first I want to say thanks and well done to all of you. I'm not sure what happened here last night but it was good to see that all of you rallied to the cause so to speak. I've arranged for agency staff to come and cover here tonight as, to be honest, we could all do with some rest. I will need a few of you to stay behind just for the changeover. Marie, John and Will if you would be so kind. As for the rest of you, thanks once again and go home."

The sullen mood that had impressed itself upon the staff room was replaced by the joy that all working people around the world share when they are sent home unexpectedly.

"I'm sorry about this," Sally said as she gathered the three unfortunate people who would have to stay, "it won't be for long I promise, and I will make it up to you."

The three of them looked at each other and then at Sally. It was Marie who spoke for them all when she said, "don't worry about it, Sally, someone had to stay."

"Thank you. Right, I'd better go and make sure that none of the agency staff is late or lost."

The three of them watched Sally leave and with a collective sigh went to get a coffee as the rest of the staff donned their coats, grabbed their bags and headed off to their real lives and loves that existed outside of the lodge. All too soon they were alone.

To busy herself as they waited Marie set about cleaning up the empty cups and wiping down the sides of the staff room.

"if you're doing that," Will said, "I'll dry up while we wait."

The three of them were only just finishing their drinks when Sally returned and said, "Alright, the agency people are here, and as luck would have it a few of them have worked here before, so it shouldn't take you long to talk them through what they have to do."

John, Marie and Will put down their cups and followed Sally out of the staff room and into the old schoolroom where she split the agency staff into three teams.

Will took the two agency cleaners assigned to him to his cleaning closet.

"Right," he said, as he passed out brooms and buckets and other cleaning paraphernalia.

"We know what to do you know," said one, a rather sullen-looking man by the name of Steven Crofter, "it's only cleaning, not rocket science."

"Well done," said Will, instantly disliking the man, "I guess there's no fooling you is there."

Crofter looked at Will with anger starting to simmer in his eyes, but he said nothing else because at heart he was a coward and a bully and even though Will seemed like a quiet man, Crofter realised quickly that Will was twenty years younger than he was and an awful lot fitter.

"OK," Crofter said, forcing a smile, "what do you want me to do?"

"Sally told me that you've worked here before so just do what you did before, OK?"

"Alright," Crofter said quietly, but as he walked off, he thought, "Just wait till your back's turned sonny, then we'll see. We'll see."

Once Will had his team set to work, he went to the old schoolroom to try and call Phillip to see how things were before he went home, but as he walked down the long corridor, he failed to notice that someone followed close behind.

"Phillip?" Will said, closing the schoolroom door behind him, "Phillip are you here?"

He watched the shadows in the room closely for any sign that he'd been heard. He watched them so intently that he did not hear the door open softly behind him.

Will didn't realise that he was in danger, but others did, and it was with a terrible scream that Martha came flying out of the shadows to stand between him and Crofter. The other man had managed to get within two metres of Will and was just about to batter him with a broom handle.

Crofter let out a scream of his own, dropped his weapon and turned and ran from the schoolroom and the lodge, forgetting his jacket which lived in the staff room for years before someone threw it away.

Crofter wasn't a changed man, because some people simply can't be changed, but each time he saw Will from that day on he would cross the road or dive into a shop to avoid him, and he had nightmares for the rest of his life about the terrible apparition that he saw that night.

"Remind me never to make you angry Martha," Will said with a smile as the ghost nurse approached him.

"I hated to do that, but Crofter is a bad man. He's worked here before and pushed a nurse down the stairs because she refused his advances."

"In that case, I don't feel so bad for him now."

"He's an insect, pay him no mind. You called Phillip, what did you want?"

Something in Martha's tone told Will that something was not right.

"Has something happened to him?"

"Yes, Otto managed to take him while everything here was crazy. We only found him a few hours ago. It's the worst that Otto has done to him. The boy only just survived."

"But Phillip told me that Otto was going to be asleep for at least a few days."

"That was a trick, just to lure poor Phillip away from me and safety. We all thought that Otto would sleep after causing so much pain, but he wanted Phillip to finish off his meal."

"You make him sound like a dessert."

"That's how Otto sees the children, just so much delicious food to be taken whenever he wants."

"This has to end, Martha, there must be some way to beat him."

"We've tried but nothing we do seems to make any difference. We even know how to beat him, but we can't."

"You know how to beat him?"

"Yes, Otto told us himself. He is so powerful, so confident; it appeals to his appetites to have given us the information knowing that we are powerless to stop him."

"But surely he's lying, you know, just playing some kind of twisted game?"

"No, it's the truth. He knows we can't win"

"What did he tell you?"

Martha thought for a moment then repeated what Otto had told her so many years ago.

"On the darkest of days with night in the afternoon, if you find my soul and take it beyond the threshold of the lodge I will be destroyed."

"The darkest of days, what does that mean?"

"It took us years to work it out. The darkest day is December the twenty-first, the winter solstice. But as to where his soul is hidden who can say?"

Will opened his mouth to speak but Martha held up a hand.

"Marie's coming," she said.

A moment later the door opened, and Marie walked in. Will was no longer surprised by Martha's disappearing act, in fact, this time he welcomed it. He was simply too tired to explain.

"How are we getting home?" she asked.

At first, Will didn't know what she meant and then it dawned on him that both had taken taxis to work

"That's a good question. Tell you what, I'll ring Brian, he might come and pick us up."

"Do you want to phone him now then? Sally has just told me that we can leave."

"OK, my phone's in the staff room."

"You go and do that, and I'll put your cleaning things away for you."

"Alright, I'll see you in the staff room."

"OK," Marie said, and watched him leave.

She smiled to herself and started to gather Will's cleaning equipment. She didn't notice a shadow move behind her, or Otto stepping from it. The monster who had caused so much misery and pain smiled at Marie's back, and just as silently as he had arrived, he stepped back into the shadows and vanished.

Will couldn't get any reception on his phone in the staff room, so he walked out into the car park and dialled his brother-in-law's number.

"Hi, Brian."

"Hello, Will, what can I do for you?"

"A lift home would be great."

"You want a lift home? Why, didn't things go well with Marie?"

"They went fine thanks, but we're at work. There was an emergency, and we had to get a taxi so could you do us a favour and come and pick us up?"

"Sure, no problem, but it's going to take about twenty minutes to get there."

"That's fine, Bri, see you soon."

By the time Marie arrived in the staff room, Will was making yet another cup of tea.

"I think I live on this stuff," she said as she took the cup of hot steaming liquid from him.

"I know what you mean," Will said, "if I ever have an operation it won't be blood they transfuse it will be hot, sweet tea."

"Did you call Brian?"

"Yes, he should be here in about twenty minutes or so."

"Good because I need to get home and have a shower. A long, hot shower."

Before Will could voice the idea that had popped into his head at the mention of Marie in the shower, John walked into the staff room.

"Are you two still here?" he said.

"No cars, John," Will answered, and started to prepare a third drink, "my brother-in-law is coming to pick us up."

"What, the pair of you?" John said, smirking. "How cosy."

"Calm yourself down big boy," Marie said to the older man. "It's just a lift home. Don't read too much into things, you'll go blind."

The three of them laughed and continued to chat while they drank their tea as Will and Marie waited for Brian to arrive.

Eventually, Will's phone rang.

"Hello?" he answered.

"I'm outside, Will," Brian said, "so get your arse in gear and let's go."

"Alright, Bri, we'll be right there."

Will hung up the phone and picked up his and Marie's jackets.

"Hang on," John said, "I'll walk with you."

As they walked past the manager's office on their way out, Sally appeared coat in hand.

"You three off now?" she said as she locked her office door.

"If that's OK?" Marie asked.

"Yes of course it is. I'm just so grateful that you all agreed to stay. It was such a big help."

Brian was standing by his car when the four of them came out.

"Hi, Will," he said, "Hi, Marie, did you enjoy the party?"

Sally and John looked at one another and then at Marie who hung her head in the sad recognition that her carefully created secret was now blown wide open.

"Yes, I did, Brian, I did."

Then looking at Sally and John, she said, "Yes OK, you were right. But can you blame me for trying to keep it secret? You know what this place is like."

Before either Sally or John could answer her there was a sudden shout from the back of Brian's car.

"Uncle Will!"

Will walked over to the car and leant through the passenger window. "Hi, J, how you doing? Hi, Bob."

Jason's ever-present companion looked up at Will and wagged his tail enthusiastically.

"Who's this?" Marie asked as she and her two colleagues walked over to the car.

"This is J," Will said, "and that's Bob."

As Marie, John, and Sally leaned forward to look at the little boy an amazing change came over Bob. The little basset hound, who had never even barked in anger before, suddenly jumped forward to stand in front of his young master. Gone was the loveable, tail wagging, mud rolling puppy and, in its place, stood the wolf that lurks at the bottom of all dog's souls. His teeth were bared and a low hard growl rose from the bottom of his throat.

"Hey, Bob," Brian said, "Get down!"

Not even the harsh, raised voice of the big man could make the dog back down. If anything, his growl became deeper and more threatening, and even the small hairs on the back of his neck were raised and stiff. It was only when the three people who had come near Jason backed away that Bob stopped his growling. The further they backed up the more he became his old self.

"I've never seen him do anything like that," Brian said as he got back into the car. "Hey, Bob, you alright?"

Bob's answer was to jump up and lick at the big man's face.

"He seems OK now," Will said.

"As entertaining as it is watching your dog go nuts," John said, heading towards his car, "I'm off."

"Yes, me too," Sally said, giving both Brian's car and the dog inside a wide berth. See you all tomorrow."

"You two ready then?" Brian said.

"You sure he's alright, Will?" Marie said nodding towards Bob.

"Yes of course he is, but if it makes you any easier you get in the front, and I'll get in the back with J and Bob."

"Alright then, but you get in first."

Will smiled at Marie's apprehension but kept it to himself. He opened the car door and got in beside his nephew and the dog.

When Marie saw that Bob didn't try and rip Will's throat out, she felt a little easier, but it was still with caution that she climbed into the front passenger seat next to Brian.

"Hello," said Jason happily, "my name's Jason and this is Bob."

"Hello, my name's Marie."

"Say hello Bob," Jason said to the basset hound.

Bob looked at Marie for a moment then he tilted his head to the left and raised his paw in a lopsided, comic salute.

"Oh, that's so cute," she said, laughing.

"He knows lots of tricks," Jason said, glad that the pretty lady was impressed with his dog.

"I bet he does,"

The journey to her flat was one of the nicest that Marie could ever remember. The four of them sang songs and Jason had Bob do some small tricks until his father stopped him.

"We don't need to be crashing son," Brian had said, smiling, "your mother would beat us both."

Jason had laughed at the thought of his mum ever raising a hand to him, but he still stopped the basset from jumping up and made him sit quietly between him and Will.

Twenty minutes later Brian was dropping Marie and Will outside Marie's flat.

"Thanks, Bri," Will said as he closed the car door, "I'll come by and pick up my car later, OK?"

"No problem, buddy."

"Bye Uncle Will," Jason said shouting out of the car window, bye Marie."

The young couple stood and waved at the departing car and then went up the stairs to Marie's front door.

"I hope you're not too mad at Brian for letting the cat out of the bag about us, Marie?"

"No, not really, it had to come out sooner or later. It would just have been nice for it to have been later, that's all. Anyway, forget about that, are you hungry?"

"Yes, actually I am."

"Well, why don't we order a takeaway, I could murder a curry."

At the mention of the rich Indian food, Will felt his stomach rumble.

"Great, do you have a menu? I'll phone up and get it delivered."

"Later," she said, "first I'm going to have that shower I promised myself."

Will watched her walk out the door. He thought about following but was unsure how she would react. Sure, they'd spent the night together but what did that mean? He was still trying to decide what to do when Marie's voice came floating into the room and dispelled all his doubts.

"Are you coming, Will?"

Chapter Seventeen

For the second time in as many nights, Will woke with Marie wrapped around him. The feel of her so close to him, the gentle brush of her breath on his neck and the way she smelled made feelings rise inside him that he had never experienced before. He felt bad that he had to keep from her what was happening at the lodge, but even though his affection for her was growing stronger and deeper each day, there was a part of him that had to admit Phillip might be right. What if by some slim chance Marie was the one helping Otto? What if all that he had experienced with her was nothing but a lie, just some way for Otto to get under his defences?

Then, quite suddenly and unbidden, the image of what had happened as they had left the lodge crept into his mind.

"Bob. Of course, Bob."

"That does a girl's confidence no good you know," Marie said looking up at him, "shouting out someone else's name while you're in bed with her, especially when it belongs to your nephew's dog."

"No, you don't understand. Bob likes you; he didn't bark. He likes you. Marie, I know this is strange but if you just trust me for a while I will explain everything. Can I borrow your car?"

"I guess so," she said as she leaned out of bed, grabbed her jeans and fished around in the pockets for her car keys, "although I don't know what's going on."

"Don't worry, Bob likes you, that's what counts?"

"How lucky am I, Bob likes me," Marie said as she watched her new lover race out of her bedroom.

Will was out of Marie's flat and in her car in a flash. The town's streets were almost empty so early in the morning, so he had no trouble getting to the lodge.

He couldn't believe he hadn't seen it before. There were three of them by the car when the dog went crazy, but when Marie got in Bob just licked her and acted like the same old puppy. He sensed something, something bad, but not with Marie because he liked her once John and Sally left.

Will nodded hello to a few of the people that he recognised and walked quickly to the old schoolroom. As soon as he was through the door he called urgently for Phillip and Martha.

The seconds passed agonisingly slowly as he waited for an answer, and just as he was just starting to think that no one was going to show the shadows in front of him shimmered and both Phillip and Martha stepped out.

"What's wrong?" Martha asked, her voice full of concern, "what's got you in such a state?"

Will took a deep breath and gathered his thoughts and then told the two of them what had happened in the parking lot. He couldn't help but smile as he watched their expressions change, it was good to see the hope that blossomed there.

"Are you sure?" Martha said, "are you sure?"

"Yes, I am. You should have seen Bob, he went crazy. There was no way that anyone was going to get near Jason, Bob would have taken their hand off. Yet when Marie got in the car, he was just soppy old Bob the basset again."

"Then it must be either John or Sally," said Phillip quietly, "but how do we find out which one it is?"

"I've been thinking about that as well," Will said with a smile, "but I want to ask you a favour. I want to tell Marie everything, and I do mean everything; Otto, you, everything."

"I don't know, Will," Martha said shaking her head, "what if you're wrong?"

Before Will could say anything, Phillip turned to Martha and said, "I say we do it. I'm tired of all this, let's take a chance and trust Will. Let him tell his girlfriend everything. What have we got to lose?"

Martha looked at the ghost of the young boy in front of her. Phillip had suffered more than anyone at the hand of Otto Crabtree. If he was willing to trust Will, then perhaps she should listen.

"Alright," Martha said, smiling at Phillip, "tell Marie what you will."

"Thank you," Will said letting out a small sigh of relief, "I know I'm right; I just know it. I want to bring her here to meet you."

Martha and Phillip looked at each other, a swift but silent discussion passing between them.

"Alright, we'll meet her," Phillip said.

"Excellent. Tonight, at tea break, I'll bring her here."

Will left the schoolroom and ran to Marie's car. As he drove back across town, he wondered how to start telling Marie about everything that had happened. Did he just blurt it all out or skirt around the issue until she guessed what he was getting at. Either way, he'd look like a raving mad man. As he pulled up outside her flat, he knew that there was only one way to do it. She might not like him afterwards, but he would have to take that chance.

He walked up the stone stairs and pressed the intercom button.

"Hello?"

"It's me."

"Hang on, I'll be right down."

Before he could say any more the intercom went dead.

"I'll just wait here then."

A few moments later Marie appeared at the front door. She had showered and changed into a pale pair of tight blue jeans and a simple white t-shirt. Her hair was tied in a soft ponytail and hung over her right shoulder.

"You look fantastic," he said as she took her car keys from him and walked down the stairs.

"You're only saying that to try and get me back into bed," she said as she unlocked her car.

"Is it working?"

"Maybe."

"Great. By the way, where are we going?"

"To get your car so that I don't have to chauffeur you about all day. Phone your sister and tell her we are on our way."

After he finished talking to his sister he turned to Marie.

"Aren't you going to ask me where I went this morning or what all that was about?"

"No, I don't own you. If you want to tell me you will, but that's up to you."

"I will tell you but not just now if that's alright."

"That's fine. What did Max say?"

"She said she's looking forward to meeting you again."

"And me her. I've got lots of questions."

"What kind of questions?" Will asked nervously.

"Now now, you have your secrets, and I have mine. That's fair, isn't it?" Marie smiled.

"Yes of course it is."

The pair of them travelled the rest of the way in companionable silence. As they pulled up outside the house Jason appeared at the front door with the ever-present Bob looking out from between his legs.

"it's uncle Will," the young boy shouted back into the house as he dashed out to the roadside.

"Hi J," Will said, catching the young boy in mid-jump and swinging him round in a full circle before putting him back down on the ground. Then it was Bob's turn, and he sprawled out on his back waiting for his belly to be rubbed.

"Come on Marie," Will said as he knelt beside the expectant dog.

"I don't know, he didn't seem very happy yesterday."

"Bob's alright," Jason said taking her by the hand and leading her to the prone dog. Marie knelt beside Will and very slowly reached out her hand and laid it on the little dog's stomach. As she did this Bob's left back leg began to twitch, and then his right leg joined in until it looked like the small basset hound was doing some kind of crazy, upside-down dance.

"That confirms it," Will thought as he watched her with Bob, "it's not her, I was right."

"If you two have finished," said Max from the doorway, "there's some coffee here for you. And there's some chocolate cake for you J."

The little boy was gone so quick it was almost like he had never been there, and of course, as soon as the boy was gone his four-legged shadow followed straight after.

"Are those two joined at the hip?" Marie said as she stood up.

"More than that," Will answered, "sometimes I think they might be twins."

"Here are your keys Will," Brian said as they walked into the kitchen.

"Thanks."

"Did you have a good time at the party, Marie?" Max asked as she put a steaming mug of coffee down on the table.

"Yes, I did thanks, a really good time." Marie answered as sipped at her coffee, "Actually, Max, there is something I wanted to talk to you about. Can we have a word in private?"

"Of course, bring your coffee we can go into the garden."

"What's all that about?" Brian asked as he watched the two women walk past him.

"To be honest, Brian I don't know," Will said, "but I tell you what, I don't like it."

"What can I do for you?" Max said as they sat down at the large wooden table that served as a centrepiece of the beautifully manicured garden.

"Wow," Marie said looking around her, "This is amazing."

Max didn't respond, she just sat there and waited for the other woman to start talking.

"I know I don't know you very well Max, but I don't know who else to ask. Is Will seeing someone else?"

Max looked at Marie for a long moment and then quite suddenly burst into laughter.

"Will cheat on someone, that's a good one."

"I didn't mean it to be funny."

"Oh, I know you didn't darling, but you see my brother just wouldn't know-how. He's not got a deceitful bone in his body, and anyway, he knows if he did, I'd make his life hell."

"Thanks, Max, that makes me feel so much better."

"Why do you ask? I mean there must be a reason."

"It's just he's been acting so strange, and he keeps calling out to someone called Martha in his sleep. And this morning he jumped out of bed talking some nonsense about it not being me and that it's alright because Bob likes me."

"Will's always been a little strange, but nothing to worry about. Anyway, what does it matter, you've only been together a little while."

Max then saw the look in the other woman's eyes and understood instantly.

"Oh, it's like that is it?"

"Yes, it is, I don't know what happened or how but there's nothing I can do about it now. I'm falling in love with him big time. You won't say anything will you?"

"No, I won't say anything. But don't forget Will might be strange but he's not stupid. Also, he's my little brother. I won't let him hurt you, but, and this is important, I won't let you hurt him either."

"Don't worry I won't hurt him. Not unless he asks me too."

Both women were laughing when Brian and Will came out into the garden.

"This is never a good sign," Brian said as he watched his wife and Marie hug each other.

"Time to go," Will said looking at his watch, "if we don't go now, we're going to be late."

The pair of them said their goodbyes and got into their cars.

"What was all that about?" Brian asked as he watched them drive away.

"She asked me if Will is cheating on her," Max answered and put her arm around her husband's waist.

Brian started to laugh.

"What, Will? That's rich."

"I know, that's what I told her. She also told me she's starting to fall for him."

"Well good for Will."

As Will followed along behind Marie his mind was full of what was to happen that night. How would she react? What would she make of it all? All these thoughts and more poured through his mind and it was with a heart full of conflicting emotions that he pulled into the lodge's car park.

Chapter Eighteen

"Are you alright?" Marie asked as they walked through the front door of the lodge.

"I'm fine. I guess it's just that I've not had much sleep over the past few nights."

Marie blushed a little as she said, "trust me BB, that is going to become quite a habit, so you had best get used to it."

Despite what he had to do that evening Will could not help but smile. He was after all an ordinary young man who had a beautiful young woman who wanted him. That was enough to make any man smile.

They parted company for a while as Marie went to get her night's assignment from Sally, and Will went to the staff room to get the keys for his cleaning locker and start his duties.

The start of his shift went as it always did. There might be an evil monster to beat and innocent children to rescue but Will also had to keep his job, so he cleaned, mopped and washed his way through the first part of the night. He knew that there was no way that he could get Marie to go with him to the schoolroom until well after midnight. She would be far too busy until then. His first opportunity to speak to her came at tea break.

"Good night, Will?" John asked as he passed the younger man a cup of tea.

Will considered the idea of John being Otto's accomplice as he took the cup.

"Nothing special, what about you?"

"Oh yes, I'm having a great shift," John said, snorting a laugh, and walked away to talk to some of the other staff.

A moment later Marie entered the room. She walked over to where Will was standing and poured herself a coffee.

"John's not trying to wind you up again, is he?" she asked.

"Not really, he just asked how my night is going, that's all."

"Well, next time he asks just think of me and remember that he has to shower alone."

Will grinned. As their previous evening ran through his mind

"Is there any way you can meet me later?" he asked quietly.

"Why?" she asked, a half-smile playing across her lips.

"I just thought it might be nice."

"Yes, alright then. Where and when?"

"What about the old schoolroom at three? It should be quiet by then."

"OK, I'll see you then."

The hours passed slowly, and it seemed to him that the closer the hands of his watch got to three a.m. the slower they went, until it felt to him that time had almost stopped completely.

Will went over his plan for what seemed like the hundredth time when Marie finally walked in. She smiled at him as she shut the door.

"So, what did you want to see me about?"

Will took her in his arms and drew her close. Over her shoulder, he saw the now-familiar shimmering in the shadows that stood in the far corner.

"I'm sorry Marie, he said holding her tight, "please try not to be afraid."

She stepped back from him when he said this and looked him square in the eye. Then slowly she followed his gaze and saw Martha, Phillip and the other lost children step slowly out of the shadows.

The scream that roared up her throat was stifled by Will's hand.

"Please, Marie, they only want to talk to you. Please trust me."

"Let her go, Will," Martha said softly, her eyes full of compassion for the young woman in front of her, "If she wants to run, we don't have the right to stop her."

The moment Marie was free of Will's arms she raced headlong for the door. She was almost through it when she realised that nothing and no one was chasing her.

"Please just listen," Will called after her as she hesitated.

Marie wanted to run. She wanted to run more than she had wanted anything in her life. But she didn't. She didn't know why then, and she didn't know why years later whenever that night came back to her. All she knew was that something had held her there for a moment, long enough to look past the shock at what she had seen, a moment to realise that what she was seeing was just a group of young, very young children, their faces haggard and afraid. But even that might not have been enough if Margery had not stepped forward at that point, waved and said, "You're pretty."

Marie let out a short laugh and despite her fright, said in return, "so are you."

And that was all it took. Marie closed the door and walked back into the room. She was still afraid but the look on the little girl's face had pulled at her heart.

"Thank you for coming back," Martha said with a smile, "Will told us you were someone special, and it looks like he was right."

Marie looked from the long-dead nurse to Will.

"You said that?"

"Yes, he did," Martha said before Will could answer, "that, and an awful lot more besides."

"We think he likes you," Margery said with the total innocence of the very young where such things are concerned.

"He does, does he?" Marie said, kneeling so that she was the same height as Margery.

"That's enough, Margery," Martha said quietly, "we have to talk about other things now."

"I'm sorry, Martha," said the little girl as she walked over to stand with her friends.

"You're, Martha," Marie said, at last realising why Will had been calling out her name in his sleep.

"You've heard of me?"

"Kind of. Will's been calling out your name in his sleep."

"Martha," Phillip said urgently, "we must hurry. Otto won't sleep forever."

"Yes, Phillip," Martha said to the young boy, "Marie, will you listen to me?"

Marie nodded her head, unsure if she wanted to hear what Martha had to say.

"Very well. All of this started when Crabtree Lodge was first built."

Twenty minutes later Martha finished her story. She had told Marie all about Otto and the monster that he was, about the children who were trapped in the lodge, and about Will and why she had chosen him.

"I can't believe it," Marie said sitting down on an old packing case.

"It's all true," Will said, sitting down beside her, "I didn't believe it myself at first, not until I heard Otto's voice the night that Joan died."

"He killed Joan?"

Both Martha and Will nodded slowly.

"He killed that poor sweet old lady just for fun?"

Again, Martha and Will nodded.

That was the turning point for Marie. Martha's story was almost just that for her, a story. But the murder of her favourite patient was something else.

"Alright, what would you like me to do?"

"Help me find out who's helping Otto," Will answered.

"Do you have any idea who that might be?" Marie asked, but before he could answer she said, "Of course, Bob."

Will smiled, and repeated, "Bob."

"So, it's either Sally or John."

"Yes, I think so, I've never seen Bob act like that before and when you got in the car, he was fine."

"So, you only decided to trust me because of a dog?"

"Please don't blame him, Marie," Martha said, "it was me who told him that we were unsure of you. But it was Will who convinced me that you could be trusted and that you would be a true asset to our cause."

Marie looked at Will for a while before responding.

"Alright, I forgive you. How do we find out which one of them it is?"

"I've had an idea about that," Will said, with an enormous sense of relief that Marie had taken things so well.

"It will have to wait," Phillip said fear starting to appear in his voice, "I can feel Otto stirring and it would be best if he didn't know that we had allies."

"Yes alright," Will said, "give me a few days and I should know who's helping him."

Without another word, Martha and the children walked back into the shadows but just before they disappeared back into the in-between Margery stopped and waved quickly at Marie.

Marie waved back and then watched as the little girl disappeared.

"What's your plan?" Marie said to Will now that they were alone.

"I'll tell you about it later, this place tends to make you paranoid. You never know who might be listening."

Marie looked around the now empty school room with new eyes.

"Yes, point taken. We'll talk later."

"Thank you, Marie. Thank you for helping."

"What else could I do? Apparently, you like me."

With that Marie turned on her heel and walked out of the room.

"You have no idea," Will said under his breath and followed behind her.

The rest of the shift passed in relative quiet for Will. Sometimes he would catch sight of a shadow moving the wrong way or a curtain wafting when there was no wind, but none of these things bothered him because he knew it was just his friends watching over him. Ever so slowly the night gave way to dawn and at last, he could put away his cleaning equipment and be on his way.

Marie caught up with him in the staff room.

"All ready to go?" she asked.

"You bet."

"Good," she said, and started to walk away,

"because I've got a surprise for you."

Will followed her out into the corridor.

"What is it?"

"I've swapped your day off."

"You did what?"

"Please don't be mad, I just thought it might be nice to spend the day together tomorrow."

"Yes, it would be, I'd like that a lot. But there is something I've got to do on my day off."

"Of course," she said, understanding his cryptic statement completely.

"If you come back to my place, I'll make you breakfast and tell you my idea."

Marie got in her car and followed him out of the car park. If either of them had glanced back at the lodge they might have seen a shadowy figure watching them from one of the downstairs windows. A few moments later John and Sally walked out of the lodge.

"Those two seem to be getting close, don't they?" Sally said smiling.

"Yes," John answered softly, "don't they."

Chapter Nineteen

"What's your plan?" Marie asked as she sipped the coffee that Will had made for her, "you're certain it's either Sally or John then?"

She had known both people for years and it was hard for her to believe that either one of them could be involved in such terrible events.

"It has to be, why else would Bob have reacted as he did?"

Marie wanted to say that there were a thousand reasons why his nephew's dog could have reacted so badly, but in her heart, she knew that she would only be looking for excuses for her friends.

"Alright," she said with a resigned sigh, "what do you want to do?"

"I was going to do this alone on my day off but as you're in this now. I guess there's no reason why we can't do it together today. I want to take Bob and Jason out and try and bump into either Sally or John and see what happens. If Bob is just his normal self, then fine but if he's not then we'll know."

"Doesn't sound like much of a plan?"

"I know, but if you can think of a better way, I'm more than willing to listen."

Marie just shook her head.

"Shame, well as you know them both, where do you think is the best place to bump into one of them?"

Marie thought for a moment before she answered.

"Sally's a workaholic, she's always at the lodge. I think our best bet is John."

"OK so how do we meet him by accident?"

"John's a bit regimented with his time off, you must have heard us ribbing him about it at work. He has breakfast at a little café in town at ten in the morning, then he goes and reads the papers in the library for a bit, and then it's back to the café for lunch and then home."

"Exciting," Will said sarcastically.

"Don't be horrible, Will. He's old and he's alone and he's not the easiest person to make friends with, but until now I thought he was harmless."

"Maybe he is and maybe he isn't. Bob will let us know for sure."

"So how do we get Bob?"

"That's the easy part; we just go and get J. I take him out on my days off quite a lot, Max won't think anything of it and where J goes, Bob goes too."

"But won't that be dangerous for Jason? I mean if John is the one helping Otto."

"I don't think so. J will be with us in the middle of a crowded town centre. And anyway, don't you remember how Bob behaved when he first met you, John and Sally?"

Marie thought back to how the loveable little dog had suddenly become a fierce and fearless guardian.

"Alright, I guess nothing's getting past Bob. When do we pick him up?"

"I usually get him about ten anyway when I take him out, so I'll phone Max and tell her."

While Will went to phone his sister, Marie busied herself in the kitchen making them both breakfast. By the time he came back into the kitchen, she had bread in the toaster, bacon under the grill and eggs in the frying pan.

"Wow," he said when he saw the hive of industry that his kitchen had become, "you'll make someone a hell of a wife someday."

"Is that an offer?" Marie said turning around and looking at him with a spatula in her hand.

"No, I mean, I was, err," Will mumbled.

"It's alright Will, I'm joking."

They sat and ate breakfast, the pair of them thinking about Will's offhand comment. They both knew something was growing between them but neither wanted to be the first to say anything about it and so, like so many other couples in the very early stages of their relationships they talked about everything and anything else until it was time to go and pick up Jason.

When they pulled up at Max's house Jason was already waiting by the gate with the ever-present Bob in tow.

"Uncle Will, Uncle Will!" he shouted excitedly.

"Hi, J," Will said getting out of the car, "what are you all dressed up for?"

"Because I'm going out with you," Jason said jumping up and down.

"Are you?"

"Mum, he's doing it again."

"You just tell him he's fibbing darling," Max called from inside the house.

"You're fibbing," Jason said pointing at his uncle, "you're a big fibber."

"Right, I'll get you for that."

The little boy let out a high-pitched scream of laughter and ran back into the safety of his home with Bob jumping up at him, barking happily.

"This is going to be some day," Marie thought and followed them both into the house.

Once inside she was ushered into the kitchen by Max while Will went with Jason to get his shoes and coat on.

"So," said Max as they sat down at the small kitchen table, "how are you and Will getting on? Do you still think he's cheating on you?"

Marie could hear the defensive tone in Max's voice and was secretly pleased that she would not have to lie to this woman who was fast becoming a friend.

"No, I was just being silly."

"About what?" Will said, walking into the kitchen.

"Nothing that you need to know about BB," Max said, getting up and making sure that Jason's coat was done up.

"Sounds juicy," Will said, smiling at Marie.

"Juicy," Jason said, imitating his uncle.

The three adults burst into laughter which in turn had Jason laughing and Bob barking, the kitchen became alive with the sounds of a happy family.

"OK then, J," Will said clapping his hands together, "let's get going."

"Are you sure you want to take Bob as well?" Max said as she walked the three of them to the door.

"It's no problem," Will said and bent down to stroke the small dog, "J will have more fun if Bob comes along."

"Bob will be fine, Mum," Jason said hopping from one foot to the other, impatient to be off.

"You make sure he is young man, and you make sure you behave for Uncle Will alright?"

"Don't worry, Max," Will said as he walked out of the door, "he'll be fine, he always is. I'll bring him back for dinner this evening."

Max waved the four of them off and when she had watched Will disappear out of sight, she stood there wondering what to do with her impromptu free time. A sudden smile broke out on her face, and she fished in her pocket for her mobile phone. She dialled her husband's number and when he answered she spoke in her sexiest voice.

"Brian, why don't you come home for lunch?"

Into town, Jason bombarded Marie and Will with question after question.

"Where are we going? Are we there yet? What are we having to eat?"

"It's a surprise J," Will said over his shoulder, "but today will involve ice cream, OK?"

"Alright, did you hear that, Bob? Ice cream!"

Bob didn't answer he just licked Jason's face happily.

Really Will had no idea where to take Jason and Bob, all the way into town he'd been racking his brain to come up with something. They needed the little dog, but they couldn't just take the pair of them home once they'd intercepted John. As they pulled up at a set of traffic lights both Will and Marie saw a poster stuck on a shop window across from them. They looked at each other and smiled and silently agreed that that was the thing to do with Jason and Bob for the day.

"Do you want a clue, Jason?" Marie said, turning round in her seat to look at the little boy.

"Yes please, Uncle Will's a meanie, he never gives me clues."

"Meanie," Marie said and stuck her tongue out at Will.

Jason laughed which had Bob barking again.

"Alright here's your clue. Where we're going you can eat cotton wool."

Jason looked at Marie with a puzzled expression.

"You can't eat cotton wool, Marie, that's silly."

"But what if it's something that looks like cotton wool?"

"Looks like," Jason said, his forehead wrinkled with the effort of trying to work out Marie's clues.

"Yes. What can you eat that looks like cotton wool?"

The wrinkles on Jason's forehead became deeper until suddenly he smiled and shouted, "Candy floss! The fair, we're going to the fair!"

"Well done, but first we'll go and have something to eat, and then to the fair after so that we can spend all your uncle's money."

"I'm paying then, am I?" Will said scowling at Jason through the rear-view mirror. The young boy just burst into laughter.

"You're funny Uncle Will."

The three of them drove the rest of the way into town talking excitedly about the fair and what they would do when they got there, but always at the back of Will's mind was the fact that first and foremost they were on the hunt for a monster, someone who was helping to keep the lost souls of Crabtree Lodge in purgatory. He parked in a small car park near the entrance to the pedestrian precinct and they all set off hand in hand to have something to eat.

"That's the place," Marie said pointing to a small café across the road from where they were standing.

Will looked at his watch.

"He should be in there now?"

"Yes, so we need to find somewhere to wait for him to leave."

Will looked around for somewhere to wait. He smiled when he saw the name of the shop just across the road from the café where John was hopefully having his breakfast.

"Do you want some cake, Jason?" Will asked pointing to the shop that was called coffee and cookies.

"I'm not allowed cake during the week. Mum says it's not good for me."

"I won't tell her if you don't, what about you, Marie?"

Marie didn't say anything, she just pretended to zip up her mouth and lock it and then throw away the imaginary key.

The little boy laughed and said, "I won't tell Uncle Will, I promise."

"In that case let's go."

They had to leave Bob tied to a small hook just outside the door. Jason wasn't very happy about this but cheered up when Will let him feed the little basset a doughnut.

Marie and Will took a table that sat in the middle of the big bay window. They drank coffee and ate a slice of cake each while listening to Jason talk excitedly about the fair. Each time the door of the café opened both turned expectantly, but it took twenty-five minutes and six strangers going in and out before John finally made an appearance.

"Will," Marie said nodding her head towards the café.

"Alright, Jason," Will said, getting up and hurriedly paying the bill, "time to go to the fair."

The three of them hurried out of the coffee shop, untied Bob and crossed the road just as John walked in front of them.

"Hello, John," Marie said, surprise held convincingly in her voice.

"Hello, you lot," John answered, but stepped back when he saw Bob standing in front of him. "I hope you've got that dog under control."

"My dog's nice mister," Jason said looking up at John, "honest he is."

John looked down at Jason, sudden thoughts of a son he didn't see any more and a grandchild he would never see flooded into his mind.

"I'm sure he is," John said as he knelt to look Jason in the eyes, "what's his name?"

"His name's Bob. Say hello Bob."

Bob sat down, tilted his head to one side and offered his right paw to John. The old man laughed as he shook the small dog's paw.

"What else can he do?" John asked, smiling.

As Jason went through his routine of tricks with Bob, Will looked at Marie and the same thought passed between them. "Sally."

Chapter Twenty

Thirty minutes later Will, Marie, Jason and Bob were walking through the middle of the fair. Will and Marie had agreed to put off their conversation about what Bob had shown them and its implications until after they had taken Jason home.

The fair was just what they needed to take their minds from the business they had become embroiled in at the lodge. They took turns taking Jason on the rides. First Will went with him on the dodgems, and then Marie took him on the carousel. Each time they went around Jason would shout and wave at Will and Bob, and Will would wave back and Bob would strain at his leash. At lunchtime, Jason got a burger and fries and Bob got a hot dog, which seemed to Will to be almost as large as the beagle himself.

"Do you want candy floss as well, J?" Will asked as the young boy finished the last of his coke.

"I'm not allowed sweets in the week Uncle Will," Jason said sadly.

"Remember what I said earlier, J, if you don't say anything then neither will we."

Jason broke into a huge smile and that was all the answer Will needed.

"Candy floss it is," he said, taking hold of Jason's hand and heading to the candy floss stall. As the three of them ate their sweet cotton wool Marie wandered over to the ghost train.

"Are you two going on this as well?"

"What do you say, J;, do you want to go on the ghost train?"

"Yes please, I love ghosts."

"Alright then, as soon as the candy floss is gone."

"All gone," Jason said immediately, opening his mouth as wide as he could to show that it was empty.

"In that case let's go."

"Have fun," Marie said as she struggled to hold on to her and Will's candy floss and a very excited Beagle.

"Don't worry about us," Will called back as he sat down in the ghost train car, "I think you should worry about how you're going to get untangled from Bob's leash."

He couldn't help but laugh as he saw Bob run around Kate's legs until she dropped the candy floss and fell on her bottom.

The car jolted into motion and bumped through the black doors to start the ride. The next thing he saw was a huge skeleton as it loomed out of the darkness. Jason screamed as a bony hand brushed the top of his head. The ride was brilliant; it had everything that a truly good ghost ride should have and more. There were ghouls and zombies, vampires and werewolves. Will and Jason laughed and screamed all the way through. But when they rounded the last corner of the ride Will's smile froze on his lips as he saw the figure that lay ahead of them. There leaning threateningly over the body of a helpless, bed-ridden child was Sir Otto Crabtree himself.

"It's OK Uncle Will, it's only Otto."

Will didn't realise what Jason had said at first, so shocked had he been by the image of the monster that walked the corridors of Crabtree Lodge, but once the ghost train had pulled to a stop and the pair of them had climbed out to a very sloppy greeting from Bob, Will said, "how did you know who that was J?"

"Who, Otto?" said the little boy as he started to rub Bob's belly, "Some of the kids at school told me about him. They say he's a ghost where you work. But I think that silly."

"What's going on?" Marie asked, confused by their conversation.

"There's a figure of Otto at the end of the ride," Will said trying to put a light tone in his voice so as not to frighten Jason, "and it made me jump."

"You don't have to be scared of Otto, Uncle Will," Jason said, looking up at his uncle, "he's very nice really."

Both Marie and Will felt their blood run cold when Jason said this. They looked at each other and then looked down at Jason.

"How do you know what he's like?" Will said kneeling so that he was eye level with Jason.

"I'm not meant to say," Jason said holding his finger up to his lips, "it's a secret."

"You can tell us J," Marie said kneeling as well, "we're good at keeping secrets, remember the candy floss."

Both the adults watched and waited as the young boy thought about this, then Jason smiled. "Ok, I guess I can tell you. He's my friend, we play hide and seek."

"Oh, my," Marie said, putting her hand over her mouth in shock.

"What do you mean?" Will asked, his face draining of colour.

"At night in my room, once mum and dad and Bob are asleep, me and Otto play hide and seek. But he's better than me I can never find him."

Marie and Will stood up and looked at each other, neither quite knowing what to say. Jason sensing the tension between them said, "Is everything alright Uncle Will?"

"Of course, J, what do you say we go and get another burger?"

"Yes please."

As the four of them walked off towards the nearest burger bar Will mouthed silently to Marie, "We'll talk later."

Kate nodded in reply and put her arm protectively around Jason's shoulder.

The rest of their day at the fair was spent in enjoyable abandon. For a while, both Will and Marie managed to put what Jason had said to the back of their minds.

After the burger bar, Will took Jason onto the big wheel, and then Marie took him into the hall of mirrors where he fell into fits of laughter when she walked into a clear plastic panel.

All too soon their day came to an end and Will gave a tired but happy Jason a piggyback ride to his car. Both boy and dog fell asleep on the drive home, but still Will and Marie refrained from talking about what Jason had said. When they arrived at the house Will carried the sleeping boy into the house and gently handed him over to Brian, who took his son upstairs.

"Did he have a good time?" Max said as she led her brother and Marie into the kitchen.

"Did he ever," Will said stifling a yawn, "I don't think there was a ride he didn't go on."

"Yes, that sounds like J," Max said with a smile.

"Max," Will said hesitantly.

"Yes?"

"Has J been having any bad dreams lately?"

"That's a strange question, but yes, he has. Well not exactly bad dreams, but a few times we've heard him talking in his sleep, almost like he's having a conversation. When we've asked him about it, he says it's his invisible friend he plays with at night. I just thought it's him being an only child. Why has he said something?"

"Only that he's not been sleeping and that he's been playing all night," Will said, trying his best to cover the reason for his question, "he told me that he keeps playing hide and seek."

"Yes, that what he's said to us. So, while you were out, I went to the chemist and got something to help him sleep, Brian should have given it to him before he put him to bed."

"Brian should have done what?" said the big man as he walked into the kitchen.

"Given J the stuff I got from the chemist."

"I did, but I almost had to wake him up to do it. If you hadn't insisted that he had it, I don't think I would have bothered."

"He needs to sleep, Brian, if he keeps waking up in the middle of the night and playing, how long before that becomes a habit?"

"Yes, I guess you're right, babe."

"Well look," Will said, "if you don't mind, we're bushed as well so we're going to get going."

Max and Brian walked the pair to the front door and waved them off. Will and Marie walked quickly to Will's car and after waving back at Brian and Max they got into the car and drove off.

Now alone on their drive back to Marie's flat they still didn't talk about what had happened at the fare, and after a few moments of broken conversation, they fell into an uneasy silence which was only broken by the car's radio and the background noise of the town as they drove through it.

It was only once they were safely behind the locked door of Marie's flat that either of them dared to bring up the subject that had been sparked by Jason's throw away comments.

"What do you think?" Marie asked as she took two beers out of the fridge and passed one of them to Will.

Before he answered Will took a long slow swallow of the ice-cool liquid.

"I don't know, but whatever's going on I bet you it's not good."

"But Otto can't be in Jason's room, can he?"

"I don't know, but after what I've seen over the past few months I'm prepared to take a few things on faith."

"What do we do?"

"I don't think there's much we can do tonight. But tomorrow I think we should go to the lodge and see if Martha can shed any light on what Jason said."

Marie flopped down onto the sofa and rested her feet on the low coffee table.

"Shouldn't we go and try and see her tonight?"

"No, if we go tomorrow and say that you need to get something out of the office no one will think twice, but if we turn up now on our day off looking as tired as we do then someone is bound to mention it to Sally, and that's something we don't want to happen."

"Alright, but what if something happens to J tonight?"

A dark cloud passed over Will's face as he thought about Marie's question. What could they do? Tell Max that a ghost was visiting her son at night and might try and kidnap him, or worse? Will imagined his sister's response to such a fantastic statement.

"There's nothing we can do. But if Max has given J something to help him sleep then I'm betting that not even Otto will be able to wake him up tonight."

"And what about tomorrow night?"

"Maybe by tomorrow we will know something that will be of help, and we can stop that monster from getting anywhere near J."

"I hope you're right," Marie said as she sank further into the couch.

"So do I, because I couldn't bear anything happening to little J."

"Me either," she said a little smile playing across her lips, "he's a little darling that one. He's going to be quite the heart breaker when he's older."

"Just like his uncle," Will said, trying to lift their mood.

"You're so modest."

"Isn't that why you like me?" Will said and kissed her gently on the lips.

Chapter Twenty-One

Marie and Will talked well into the night. Their conversation ranged from the latest news to what was their favourite toy as a child. They covered almost every subject apart from the one that had occupied their minds for most of the past weeks. It was as if their minds, realising there was nothing they could do for the moment, had decided to give their worn and tired bodies a few hours of blessed release. As with soldiers on the battlefield during a lull in the war, rest must be taken when it is offered because you never knew when or if it will come again.

"You know what?" Marie said suddenly, "I'm hungry, what about you?"

At the mention of food Will's stomach rumbled and he realised that apart from a rather greasy burger he'd eaten nothing but candy floss all day.

"I'll take that as a yes," Marie said smiling, "I'll go and rustle something up."

Will felt a slow burn of lust as he watched Marie's jean-clad bottom swagger seductively into the kitchen, and for a moment he thought about following her and suggesting they retreat into the bedroom instead, but another rumble from his stomach drove such thoughts from his mind.

"Is there anything I can do?" Will called out from his comfortable perch on the couch.

"You could open a bottle of wine if you like. It's in here just by the sink."

Will stretched as he stood up and walked into the kitchen, letting his hand brush gently along the small of Marie's back.

"None of that," she said with a smile, "or we won't get anything to eat."

"Where's your bottle opener?" Will said pretending not to have heard her.

"It's here," she said, pulling open the drawer in front of her, "I'll pass it to you. You seem to have a bad case of wandering hands tonight."

"I don't know what you mean."

"Yes, I'm sure you don't. Just open the wine handy, and I'll get on with cooking us something to eat."

By the time Will had opened the wine and found some wine glasses a beautiful aroma filled the small kitchen.

"That smells fantastic," Will said as he took a big breath, "what is it?"

"It's just a few bits I had laying around," she said, blushing a little. She had always lacked confidence as a cook and compliments were hard for her to take.

"Go and find us something to watch and I'll bring it over. There are some films down by the side of the TV, just pick one."

Will leafed through Marie's small collection of films as she walked in from the kitchen.

"This is some strange lot of films you've got here."

"Yes, I know, my dad loved old back and white films, and I guess I picked up the habit from him. If you don't like them there might be something on TV."

"No, I'll give them a go. Which one's your favourite?"

"Anyone, I love them all."

Will thought for a moment, but as he didn't know one from another, he closed his eyes and picked one at random.

"This one's called Carry on Teacher."

"That one's great. It's an old comedy from the fifties."

"Sounds exciting," he said as he handed her the DVD remote control and sat down beside her.

"Don't be sarcastic, it's good, you just wait and see. I bet you love it."

Will didn't care for old films, let alone ones in black and white. To him, they almost seemed like something that came out of the ark, but even before the first fifteen minutes of it were up, he found himself chuckling and enjoying the film far more than he had expected.

About halfway through the film, he noticed that Marie's breathing had slowed, and she was pressed up tightly beside him. As he sat there watching a film older than his father and with his new girlfriend sleeping beside him, Will realised that he was happier than he had been in a very long time. He looked down at her sleeping face and felt a wave of feelings for her. There was something about her, something he could not have put into words, but he would not have swapped places with anyone at that moment, and it was with a smile that he gently kissed her on the forehead, picked up his wine glass and lost himself in the film. By the time it had finished, Will's breathing had fallen in step with Marie's, and he joined her in a sweet and dreamless sleep.

He was woken by the fantastic smell of frying bacon. He stood up and stretched as Marie walked out of the kitchen. She had changed from the clothes she had fallen asleep in, to a men's large shirt that far from hiding her figure, extenuated it and gave her a sensual appeal that outweighed even the most elegant evening dress that Will had ever seen.

"Like the view?" Marie said as she caught him staring at her.

"As a matter of fact, I do."

"Yes well, don't get any ideas," she said, smiling as she put a cup of coffee into his hand and kissed him quickly on the cheek, "we've got to go to the lodge and talk to Martha."

"What time is it?"

"It's seven-thirty already. Do you want breakfast?"

"Yes please," he said and walked into the kitchen sipping his coffee.

"Sit down then, and butter that toast if you don't mind."

Will did as he was asked and by the time he had buttered two pieces of toast each, Marie put a lovely breakfast in front of him.

Once they had finished and cleared away, Marie went for a shower while Will made them both another cup of coffee. As he waited for the kettle to boil his mind filled with images of Marie, hot, soapy water cascading down her beautiful body. He was just thinking about joining her when she walked back into the kitchen wrapped in a towel, using another to dry her hair.

"Are you alright?" she asked when she saw the slight blush that had come to his face.

"I'm fine," he said, embarrassed that he'd been caught by the very woman he had been fantasising about, "nothing wrong with me."

"What were you thinking about?"

"To be honest, I was thinking about you in the shower."

"Really? Well, if you're a good boy maybe when we get back from the lodge I'll give you a live show."

Twenty minutes later the two of them were heading across town towards the lodge. The closer they got the quieter Marie became, until she stopped talking completely.

"Are you OK?" Will asked after several minutes of complete silence had passed.

"Yes, I'm fine."

"Come on, what's wrong?"

"It's Sally, it's just hit me. She's been my friend for so many years and now it turns out that I never really knew her at all. I thought she was the best friend I'd ever had and now I feel so betrayed. How long has she been playing me for a fool, pretending to be my friend when all the time she's been in league with that monster?"

Will knew that there was nothing he could say to make Marie feel better. The one person she had thought she could trust had turned out to be the one person she couldn't. How did you console someone when they realised that what they'd thought was a true friendship turned out to be a sham?

As he drove Will stole glances across at Marie and in these brief snapshots, he saw her stop crying and grow hard and cold. In a way, it was a terrible thing to see. She no longer thought of Sally as her friend and confidante, she was now the enemy. Someone putting the life of a small child in danger for their own ends.

By the time they turned into the lodge's car park and pulled over, Marie's transformation was complete. Will didn't need to ask if she was ready to go inside, he could see it in the cold, hard stare that she wore. But he asked anyway, as much to break the silence as anything else.

"Are you ready for this?"

"Let's go," she answered, and stepped out of the car.

Will joined her and after a moment's pause, the pair of them walked into the lodge to find Martha.

Chapter Twenty-Two

As Will had predicted the night before, no one paid them the slightest notice as they walked through the lodge towards the old schoolroom. They were simply part of the workforce, faces that people saw every day and very soon became invisible. If asked had they been there, anyone who saw them that morning would have had to stop and think before they answered.

When they got to the schoolroom Will blocked the door by wedging an old chair under the handle. Once he was sure it was firm he walked into the centre of the room and softly called Martha's name. They only had to wait a few moments before Martha stepped out of the shadows.

"We have some news for you," he said, stepping towards the ghostly nurse.

She didn't answer but Will could see from her expression she was hoping they were going to tell her who had been helping Otto, and he was glad to finally have some positive information for the troubled spirits of the lodge.

"We think it's Sally."

"Really?" Martha said, her voice colder than a winter's night, "Do you have proof?"

"Apart from the way Bob reacted, no. But that must be proof enough, doesn't it?"

"No, it's not," Martha said gently. She knew how much this young man wanted to help them, but she could not act on the reaction of one small dog, "we will watch Sally more closely from now on. If you are right, then it will be a very bad day for her indeed."

The implication in her words made Will's blood run cold. Martha, Phillip and the others had suffered for well over a hundred years at the hands of Otto Crabtree, and no matter what they had done Will couldn't help but feel sorry for anyone that fell into the hands of these vengeful spirits.

"What do you want us to do, Martha?"

"I think it best that the two of you do nothing at all. If Sally is in league with Otto, then we had best not give her any idea that we know."

"OK, whatever you say."

"How are you, Marie?" Martha asked, turning to look at the young woman, "I know Sally is your friend."

"Was my friend," Marie said, "was."

"You must try and hide your feelings. I know you feel betrayed, but she must never become aware of how you feel about her now. You must be as friendly and as open with her as you have always been."

"I'll try, that's all I can promise."

"That's all I can ask."

"There is something else, Martha," Will said, slipping his hand into Marie's.

"Yes?"

"My nephew told me that Otto has been playing hide and seek with him at night. But that can't be possible, can it?"

It was a few moments before Martha answered his question, and that time was all that Will needed to know that his worst fears were about to be realised.

"I'm afraid it is. This is how Otto gets into the minds and hearts of the children that end up here."

"But you said that he can't leave the lodge."

"In essence that's true, but he can project himself to other places. He can't touch your nephew in any way, but if he has visited him, then sooner or later he will lure the boy here to the lodge, and once that happens then he will belong to Otto and join the rest of us."

"But how can he do that? I can't see him walking into my sister's house and just taking J. Max would tear him apart."

"No, Otto would not do that," Martha said, a small smile crossing her lips at the thought of Otto trying to take the boy from his mother, "there is no more dangerous creature on the planet than a mother protecting her young and Otto knows that. No, his methods are far more subtle than a simple kidnapping. He will keep visiting the boy, telling him the most wonderful tales until Jason thinks of Otto as his best friend. Then one night Otto will tell the boy about the lodge and how much fun he can have, and you know what will happen then."

"We can't let that happen," Marie said, tears in her eyes, "we just can't."

"I'm not sure how we can stop it," Martha said sadly, "it's something I've seen before with the last child that Otto lured here to the lodge."

Neither Marie nor Will wanted to ask who that was, but both were interested to hear the story just in case there was some information in it that could help Jason and keep him safe. Martha could see they wanted to know, so with a sigh, she told them the story.

"Margery was the last child to be seduced by Otto. It must have been nearly seventy years ago. Her father was a doctor here at the lodge and one day he brought her to work. Once Otto laid eyes on her the poor girl's fate was sealed. A few months later little Margery sneaked out of her house late at night and came to the lodge. The poor girl's body was found right here in the schoolroom the next morning. I can still see the look of pain and despair in her parents' eyes, and that is something I never want to see again."

"There must be something we can do," Will said, his voice full of despair.

"The only thing you can do is postpone what will happen, not prevent it."

"Then I'll do that, the more time we have the better. What do I have to do?"

"What do we have to do?" Marie said, stepping to his side.

"Thanks," Will said gratefully. Her only response was to hold his hand tighter and gently rub his arm.

"The only thing you can do," Martha said, "is to make sure that the boy is never alone, especially at night."

"That's not going to be the easiest of things to do," Will said, "I mean I can't tell my sister and her husband that a ghostly monster from the lodge where I work is going to steal their son away. They'll think I'm insane."

"You must find a way," Martha said softly, "because if you don't then eventually, I will have another child to care for."

"Alright, I'll think of something. Is there anything else that we can do?"

The ghost in front of them was just about to answer when her head suddenly snapped up and she said, "Something is happening outside, something important. And I bet that Otto is at the bottom of it."

Before either of them could ask Martha what she was talking about the ghost stepped backwards into the shadows and vanished.

"What was all that about?" Marie asked, looking at Will.

"I don't know, so I suppose we should go and have a look."

The pair of them walked back through the lodge. When they got to the main doors, they found it to be a hive of activity. Medical people were milling around the main entrance and when Will glanced out of the door into the car park, he saw a virtual fleet of ambulances and police cars.

"What on earth is going on?" he asked anyone who was listening.

"We're being closed down," said Sally's voice from behind them. They both turned.

"What do you mean being closed down?" Will asked, squeezing Marie's hand tightly to remind her to keep her temper.

"Just that. All the patients are to be moved to other authorities, and the lodge is to be closed until further notice."

"But why?"

"Something was found when they carried out the autopsy on Joan. No one will tell me what it is, but all the staff are to be interviewed, and the lodge is to be searched."

"Searched for what?"

"I don't know. No one will tell me anything."

"Are you alright, Marie?" Sally asked, noticing her former friend's facial expression.

"I'm alright, Sal," Marie said, her voice never betraying her true feelings for a moment, "just a little shocked by all this."

"I know dear," Sally said, putting her arm around the other woman's shoulders.

Marie returned the gesture and hugged her former friend with all the affection she could muster.

"Excuse me, Miss Cutter," said a voice from behind the trio.

They turned to see a rather short, balding man dressed in a dark suit and carrying a slim, black briefcase.

"Ah, Mr Brown," Sally said, letting go of Marie "let me introduce the assistant head nurse."

"You would be, Miss Mallory," said Brown, looking Marie up and down, and then turning to Will, "and you would be?"

"My name's Will McCormick," said Will holding out his hand for the other man to shake.

Brown looked at the offered hand but did not attempt to take it.

"McCormick. You would be the night porter."

"Yes, that's me, and you are?"

"My name is Brown. I'm the investigating officer for the local authority. It's my job to find out exactly what happened on the night of Mrs Reedum's death."

"But why?" Marie asked, "Joan's death was an accident, wasn't it?"

"That's what I'm here to discover Miss Mallory."

"Sally said there were some discrepancies with Joan's autopsy," Marie asked, "what kind of discrepancies?"

"I'm afraid that's privileged information, Miss Mallory. But suffice to say there were enough to warrant this investigation."

"Oh, I see."

"Now as you and Mr McCormick were on duty on the night of Mrs Reedum's death I will need to interview the pair of you. Miss Cutter, can I use your office?"

"Yes of course, Mr Brown, you know where it is."

"If you two would follow me," Brown said and walked off toward Sally's office.

Will and Marie looked at each other and then followed behind Brown.

"Good luck," Sally said to the pair of them as they went.

"Do we need it, Sal?" Marie asked, looking around at her former friend.

"Just a figure of speech, that's all," Sally smiled, but once Will and Marie had turned away, her smile slipped from her face and was replaced by a scowl that turned her eyes to ice chips.

"How did I do?" Marie asked as they followed Brown.

"Better than I expected," Will said taking hold of her hand, "now let's go see what this Brown has to say for himself."

Chapter Twenty-Three

"If you'd be so good as to wait here, Mr McCormick," Brown said, pointing to an old plastic chair that stood just beside the picture of Otto Crabtree, "I'll interview Miss Mallory first."

"No problem, take your time." Will wanted to wish Marie good luck but thought better of it. He just didn't know what Brown would make of such a gesture. He watched as they walked up the corridor towards Sally's office and tried to catch Marie's eye before she walked into the office, but his view was blocked by Brown's back.

"What a dick," he whispered to the empty corridor once Brown had followed Marie into the office.

The minutes passed slowly. He found that he could only sit beside the huge picture of the lodge's founder for a little while before he had to move. He got up and slowly paced the corridor, wondering what kind of questions were being asked.

Half an hour passed before the office door opened and Marie walked out.

"Are you alright?" he asked.

"I'm fine."

Will could see that Marie was far from alright, he noticed how red her eyes were and knew that she'd been crying.

"What on earth did he say to you in there?"

"Mr McCormick," Brown said from the open office doorway, "if you would be so kind."

"I'll meet you by the car, Will," Marie said taking his hand and squeezing it quickly, "be careful."

Before he could ask her what she meant Brown called to him again.

"Mr McCormick."

"Yes, I'm coming."

Brown sat behind Sally's desk with a large A4 pad in front of him.

"Please, Mr McCormick take a seat."

For a moment Will thought about refusing the seat and telling this smiling pen pusher that he would stand. But then he realised that anger would not be the way to go with this man. Brown was looking for that kind of reaction. To him, it would almost be as good as a confession so Will gave Brown his best smile and said, "Thanks."

"Now then, Mr McCormick, you're the night porter here at the lodge. Is that right?"

"Yes, that's right."

"And what does that entail exactly?"

"Mostly cleaning, sweeping, and taking out the rubbish, that kind of thing."

"You don't have anything to do with the patients then?"

"I'm not sure what you mean," Will said, being purposely evasive.

"I mean do you have any contact with the patients, Mr McCormick?"

"Apart from saying hello when I pass them in the corridor, no."

"Can you tell me what you were doing on the night of Mrs Reedum's death?"

"My job, Mr Brown," Will said coldly, disliking the implication in the other man's voice, "cleaning, sweeping, and taking out the rubbish. That kind of thing."

"And where were you when you heard that she had died?"

"I was in the staff room having my tea break with the rest of the staff."

"Then what did you do?"

"Nothing."

"Nothing, Mr McCormick?" Brown said, looking across the table at Will, "really?"

"Yes, what did you expect me to say? I'm just the night porter, not a nurse."

"Weren't you curious, Mr McCormick?"

Will thought before he answered this question. He realised that Brown was looking for something, but he just wasn't sure what.

"Yes of course I was. Who wouldn't be, what with alarms going off and the like? But I'm not stupid, Mr Brown. If I don't get in the way then I can't get in the way, if you know what I mean."

"Yes, Mr McCormick. Well, I think that's all for now."

"I can go?"

"Yes, Mr McCormick, you can go. But I may need to speak to you again."

Will got up without another word and left the office as quickly as he could. The lodge had a hollow quality to it now that all the patients and staff were gone, and Will's footsteps echoed as he walked out of the lodge and into the sunlit car park.

"Well, he's a dick," he said as he got into the car beside Marie.

"Yes, he is."

"What did he ask you?"

"It was more like he was accusing me of having something to do with poor Joan's death."

"But that's crazy, why on earth would he do that?"

"Apparently there was an unusual substance in Joan's blood."

"What kind of substance?"

"He wouldn't tell me that." Marie glanced across at him for a moment, "the way he spoke was like he thought I'd killed her and that I already knew what he was talking about."

"But how could there have been anything in Joan's blood if Otto killed her?"

"Isn't it obvious?"

"Sally?"

"Yes, Sally. She must have injected something into Joan before the ambulance took her body away."

"But why would she do that?"

"I guess Otto wants the lodge emptied for some reason."

"You don't think it has something to do with J, do you?"

"Yes, I do. I don't know how but I'm sure it does."

"Then we have to make sure that little J isn't left alone at night."

"But how do we do that? Like you told Martha, we can't tell Max, she'll think we're insane."

"I've been thinking about that. J sometimes stays at mine for a night or two, and now the lodge is closed I could ask if he wants to stay for a week. I'm sure Max would go for it. That way we could watch him all the time."

"A week's not long Will."

"No, you're right, it's not. But at least it will give us some time to hopefully come up with something."

"What's the plan?"

"I'll call Max and tell her about what happened at the lodge. She'll ask us over for dinner, we'll have a few drinks and end up staying the night."

"And then we talk to her in the morning?"

"Not right away. We wait until J and I start being very, very loud. She's far more likely to agree if he's being a pain."

Once they were back inside Marie's flat, she made coffee while Will called Max and told her what had happened at the lodge. As he had predicted, Max invited them both over for dinner.

A few hours later they were at Max's house being greeted by a madly waving Jason and his ever-present sidekick.

"Hi, Uncle Will," Jason said and jumped into his uncle's arms.

Will responded by spinning the young boy around.

"Hi J, what have you been up to?"

"I've been to playschool today; we made a wish box."

"What's a wish box?"

"You don't know what a wish box is?" Marie asked with a smile.

Will shrugged his shoulders.

"He doesn't know what it is, does he, Marie?" Jason said, laughing as he jumped up into her arms.

"No, I don't think he does."

"Hey, you little traitor, what's this, deserting me for a woman?"

"She smells nice."

Will tried to look menacing but failed terribly.

"I think he's trying to tell you that you smell," said Marie, unable to keep the smile off her face.

"You're in real trouble now little man," Will said, making a grab for Jason's leg.

Both Marie and Jason squealed and ran into the house, closely followed by Bob, barking excitedly.

"I think Will and Marie are here," Max said to her husband.

"I don't know how you do it," Brian said, laughing at the mayhem that had just come charging through their front door, "I didn't hear them."

"Open the wine, dummy," Max said.

They had a great evening eating takeaway food and playing games, and just as Will knew she would Max invited them both to stay. They pretended to refuse but let Max and Jason beat them into submission. Once it was settled Brian poured more wine and Max helped Jason into his pyjamas.

"Cool PJs," Will said when Jason came back downstairs.

"Mum got them yesterday," Jason looked down at the muscle-bound wrestlers on the front of his pyjamas. "I liked my old ones better."

"The old one's had too many holes in them J," Max said, smiling at her son. "You know that."

"I still liked them."

"Well anyway mister, it's time for you and your new pyjamas to get off to bed."

"But mum," Jason protested, trying his best to win an unwinnable fight, "Uncle Will's here, can't I stay up for a little bit longer?"

To everyone's surprise, Jason's most of all, Max said, "Alright, but only for a little bit, OK?"

"Really?"

"Yes really, or would you like me to change my mind?"

"No, mum," Jason said giving Max a neck-breaking hug, "don't do that."

It was only twenty minutes later that Jason was yawning so hard it looked like his head was going to split in two.

"OK, J," Max said softly, "that's it now, bedtime."

Jason almost started to argue, but his mother's expression told him he wouldn't be so lucky again, "can Uncle Will take me up please?"

"Of course I can. Come on let's go."

The little boy took hold of his uncle's hand and with his sleepy dog following behind went up the stairs to bed.

"He's a lovely boy," Marie said as they disappeared.

"Jason or Will?" Max asked, quick as a flash.

"I was talking about Bob."

Brian snorted, almost choking on his mouthful of wine which in turn set the two women into fits of laughter.

"I guess you had better show Marie where she's going to be sleeping, Max," Brian said once they had regained their composure.

"Good idea, and I'll give you something to wear."

By the time Will came back downstairs, Max and Marie had changed into nightshirts.

"Sexy," he said with a smile when he saw Marie in her light pink nightshirt with a small blue teddy bear on the front and white ankle socks."

"I think so. By the way, it seems you forgot to tell me what happens when you sleep here."

"Ah, you mean me sleeping in J's room, don't you?"

"At least you get a room," Marie said, taking another glass of wine from Brian, "I get the couch."

"If it makes you feel any better all I get is a sleeping bag and a floor that I have to share with a mountain of toys."

"OK, well maybe the couch isn't so bad after all."

The four of them talked well into the night until at last Max said, "Well, I'm off to bed, some of us still have to get up in the morning."

Marie yawned and stretched.

"I think I'm ready for bed too."

Brian and Max said their goodnights and left Will and Marie in the front room. Once they had gone Will said, "I'm sorry we can't sleep together, but I always sleep in J's room when I stay here."

"That's OK BB, I'll let you make it up to me another time. Just be careful in case you-know-who turns up."

"I can't see him making an appearance with someone else being in the room, but I will."

Will kissed Marie and made his way as quietly as he could up to J's room. The little boy didn't even stir as Will unrolled his sleeping bag, undressed and climbed in. He tried to stay awake to watch over Jason, but the long day combined with several glasses of wine was just too much for him and he fell into a deep sleep in just a matter of minutes.

So, he failed to see Otto Crabtree step out of the shadows and softly whisper into his nephew's ear.

Chapter Twenty-Four

The first thing that Will saw when he opened his eyes was the early morning sun gleaming through a small crack in the curtains of his nephew's room. The second thing he saw was a large stuffed dinosaur as it flew through the air and hit him squarely between the eyes.

"Hey," he said as he picked the large purple toy up, "what's your game."

The only answer he received from Jason was another flying toy, this time a small dark brown teddy bear.

"Morning, Uncle Will," Jason said giggling as he watched the teddy bear cartwheel through the air towards his Uncle's head.

Will snatched the teddy out of the air just before it made contact with him and shouted.

"Right Mr. you're for it now."

Jason squealed and flew from his bed and out of the door before Will was even untangled from his sleeping bag.

Marie and Max were in the kitchen drinking coffee when Jason and Bob burst into the kitchen and disappeared under the table. Marie looked at Max for an explanation but all she got in return was a shrug of her shoulders and a look that suggested that this was normal behaviour for her son. So, turning from Max Marie looked under the table and said, "Are you ok, Jason?"

"Shh," the little boy said holding a finger to his lips, "we're hiding."

Marie sat up and once more looked at Max. This time the other woman said, "Don't get involved, it's always like this when Will stays."

At that moment a bare-chested Will burst into the kitchen and shouted, "Right, where are they?"

Both women shrugged their shoulders in an 'I don't know' gesture which didn't do much to convince Will that both boy and Beagle were not in the kitchen.

"I know you're here," Will shouted as he opened cupboards and drawers in his search, "and when I find you, you know what happens."

A small squeak from beneath the table followed Will's threat.

"I heard that," Will said angrily as he moved to the table and started to search the top of it, lifting plates and looking inside cups, "you must be here somewhere and when I find you it shower time for you and your little dog."

Not going in the shower," Jason said stubbornly from beneath the table.

Will knelt, lifted the tablecloth and said, "got you."

Jason screamed, Bob barked, and the pair of them dashed from beneath the table right between Will's legs and flew out of the kitchen just as quickly as they had entered it. The moment Boy and dog were through the door and out of earshot Will sat down and said, "Well that was fun, any coffee sis?"

As Max put a steaming cup of coffee down in front of her brother Marie asked, "Did you really put Jason in the shower?"

"Yes, I did and Bob too," Will said as he sipped at his coffee.

"That's cruel," Marie said as she tried to hide a smile at the thought of Will struggling with Jason and Bob to get them in the shower.

"Well don't laugh then," Will said as he stood up and went to refill his coffee cup.

"Trust me, Marie," Max said sitting down at the table, "that was nothing. Once I found the three of them in the garden at one in the morning having a water fight."

"You're joking," Marie said, a disbelieving look coming to her face

"I only wish I was," Max answered, "So as you can understand Jason hiding under the table in the morning is very minor."

When Max turned to make another pot of coffee for them all Marie glanced at Will and with a nod of her head towards Max indicated that now would be the time for Will to ask his sister about Jason staying with them

"Max," Will said to his sister's back, "I was thinking."

"Careful, BB," Max said without turning around, "we don't want that peanut of a brain of yours overheating do we."

Marie despite herself laughed at this.

"Anyway," Will said giving Marie the dirtiest look he could manage, "as I was saying. Seeing as neither Marie nor I have a job to go to at the moment I was thinking that if you wanted, we could look after J for a few days or maybe even a week. It would give you and Brian a break and you know J loves staying with me."

Will and Marie sat quietly at the kitchen table as Max thought for a moment about their offer.

"What do you think, Brian?" Max asked her husband as he walked into the kitchen and poured himself a cup of coffee.

"About what?" Brian asked as he said down at the table.

"About J staying with Marie and Will for a few days."

"I think that J would love it," Brian said, "and it might be nice to have a few days to ourselves."

"Alright," Max said to her brother, "J can stay with you. But if he gets too much you must promise to phone me and bring him back. J and that dog can be a right handful sometimes."

"Great," Will said managing to suppress his sigh of relief, "when do you want us to pick him up?"

"He's got playschool this morning," Max said thinking out her son's day, "so what about you pick him up late this afternoon, say about three."

"Aright," Will agreed, "that should give us more than enough time to get home, shower, change and then get some shopping done so that we've got things in J will like."

"You shopping," Max said to her brother, "alright where's my real brother."

"Haha," Will said sarcastically as he stood up, "everyone's a comic."

"Well just make sure you don't tell J he's going to stay with you, or he'll never go to playschool."

"Now that's tempting," Will said with an evil smile, "just imagine what kind of day you would have if I did that."

"You could also imagine the black eye you'd have if you did," Max said sternly.

"Err on that note," Marie said standing up as well, "I think we'd better go. I don't find it a turn on to watch my new boyfriend get his arse kicked by a woman half his size."

Brian almost choked on his coffee when he heard this.

"That's not funny," Will said suddenly indignant, "I can take her."

"And what happened last time you and Max got into it?" Brian said smiling the smile of someone what already knows the answer to the embarrassing question they have asked.

"I can't remember," Will mumbled.

"Oh my God, what happened?" Marie asked unable to help herself.

"I broke his nose," Max said, a self-satisfied look on her face.

"It was only dislocated," Will said, "and anyway that only happened because I didn't want to hurt you."

"Of course it did, BB," Max smiled condescendingly, "of course it did."

"Alright," Brian said stepping in between brother and sister, "we don't want you to not hurt her again do we, Will."

"Yes, come on, Will," Marie said taking him by the arm, "we have a lot to do before we pick up J this afternoon."

When they got outside to their car Marie said, "I've got to ask, how on earth did Max break your nose."

Will looked at her over the roof of the car for a moment then he said, "I was ten and Max was twelve. I stole her Barbe and when she got it back, she hit me in the face with a Mr Potato head doll. She dislocated my nose and gave me a black eye."

Will waited for Marie to say something, but she just stood there looking at him her lips pressed tightly shut and as he watched a small tear started to run slowly down her cheek.

"Oh, I'm glad I make you laugh," Will said trying to sound stern but failing miserably.

"I'm sorry," Marie said as she took a tissue from her pocket and dabbed at her eyes, "it's just I never realised that Mr Potato head needed to come with a health warning."

"Yes, very funny," Will said as he unlocked the car, "now get in the car before you wet yourself laughing."

They were well over halfway home before the last giggles had worked their way out of Marie's system.

"Finished?" Will asked when at last Marie had stopped laughing.

"Maybe," she said taking a tissue out of her pocket and dabbing at her eyes again, "but I can't promise anything."

"I've been thinking about where J's going to sleep once we pick him up," Will said, as they drove alone.

"I never thought about that," Marie said looking at him," you only have a one bet flat.

"What I was thinking is that me and J can camp out in the front room and you can have the bedroom."

"What all on my own," Marie said pouting, "what if I get lonely?"

"Then you will have to get lonely," Will said with a smile, "it's just too small a flat for that kind of thing.

"I'm sure I don't know what you mean," Marie said, in her best innocent voice, "I'm a good girl I am."

"Don't I know it," Will said with a wicked grin.

Twenty minutes later they pulled up outside Marie's flat so that she could pack some clothes for her stay at Will's.

"Anyone would think we're moving in together," Will said when he saw the size of the case that Marie appeared with.

She looked Will square in the eyes and said seriously, "would that be such a bad thing?"

Will looked back at her, thought for a moment then said, "no I don't think it would be."

"Then maybe after J goes home we should talk," Marie said as she passed her bag to Will and watched as he put it in the boot of the car.

"I think we should," he said as he closed the boot, "but for now J is what's important."

The pair of them were silent as they drove to Will's flat each shocked by the sudden development in their relationship, neither of them had been looking for anything serious but somehow each of them had pushed their way into the other's heart. Until quite by accident they found themselves in love. To try and break the ice that had grown between them Marie turned the conversation to what they would do with Jason once he was staying with them.

"I'm not sure really," Will said secretly glad that Marie had turned the conversation away from the previous subject, "I was thinking that whatever we do should be so tiring that J falls dead asleep each night. That way Otto won't get a chance to get to him."

"Alright," Marie said agreeing with him, "that sounds like a plan. So, it's the park then the zoo, maybe the pictures, lots of games and takeaways."

"Stop please," Will laughed, "I'm getting tired just listening to you."

"We have to burn up your energy somehow while J's here don't we?" Marie said putting her hand on Will's knee, "because there won't be any other way will there?"

"Well, we don't pick him up for an hour you know," Will said as he pulled up outside his flat.

"Really," Marie said, moving her hand further up Will's leg, "that's interesting."

The pair of them walked up to Will's flat hand in hand with only one thought between them. As Will unlocked his door his phone started to ring.

"Leave it," Marie whispered as she placed a kiss gently on his neck.

Will was just about to do that very thing when he noticed that it was Max who was calling.

"It's Max," Will said a strange feeling settling over him.

"I think you'd better answer it, Will," Marie said experiencing the very same sense of foreboding as Will.

"Hi, Max," Will said answering the phone to his sister.

"Will," Max said he voice shrill and frightened, "it's J, he's disappeared."

Chapter Twenty-Five

"What do you mean disappeared?" Will said, almost shouting into his phone.

"Please, Will," Max said ignoring his question, "we need you."

"What's going on," Marie asked as Will's phone went dead.

"It's Jason," Will said repeating just what Max had told him, "He's disappeared."

"I don't understand," Marie said as she followed Will back out to his car, "how can he just disappear."

"I don't know," Will said almost running down the steps of his building, "Max didn't say anymore she just asked me to get there."

Will didn't even ask Marie if she was coming with him the look on his face was answer enough. She had grown to love the little boy, and she was going to do everything that she could to help.

Will drove at breakneck speed back to Max's house and completed a journey that would have normally taken forty minutes in fifteen. When he pulled up, he saw two police cars sitting outside his sister's house.

"Oh, Will thank goodness," Max said when she saw her brother and his girlfriend.

"What happened, Max?" Will said as he walked through the front door, "and where's Brian?"

"Brian's gone in a police car to look for J just in case he's just wandered off, and they said I should stay here in case he comes home."

"I'll make a cup of tea, shall I?" Marie said as she watched Max step into Will's arms and start to cry.

"What happened, sis?" Will said softly as he held Max.

"About an hour or so after you left, we got a call from J's playschool saying that after no one had seen J since the mid-morning break."

"But don't they check to see how many kids they have?" Will asked.

"At the beginning of the day yes," Max said stepping back from her brother as she regained her composure, "but after that, all the doors are locked so that none of the children can just walk out. Even the outside play area has a high fence running around it. That's why we chose the place for J it's so secure."

"I guess they searched the school before they phoned you?" Will asked, taking a cup of tea from Marie as she walked back into the room.

"Yes," Max said sitting down and taking her tea from Marie, "they have a procedure for just this thing. You know in case a kid is just playing hide and seek that kind of thing."

At that moment Brian walked in closely followed by a policeman. Max looked up expectantly at him, but all her husband did was slowly shake his head.

"This is crazy," Max said standing up and pacing around the room, "how on earth could he have got out of the school and where could he have gone, he's only four for god's sake."

"We've talked to the staff at the place school Mrs Williamson," said the policeman stepping forward he was a slightly built young man in his early twenties call Ray Billings, "asking them if they've seen anyone loitering around the place or anything suspicious."

"What you think someone might have taken him?" Max asked her face turning very pale.

"No," answered the policeman just a little too quickly," it's just procedure that's all. That playschool is a very secure place. My friend's children go there. I'm sure that he'll turn up very soon feeling hungry and scared but none the worse for wear."

"Was there anyone lurking about the place?" Will said asking the question that his sister and Brian were afraid to ask.

"And you would be?" P.C Billings said turning his attention to Will.

"I'm Max's brother Will," Will said, "and this is Marie a friend of the family."

"You can tell them anything you can tell us, officer," Max said softly, "their family."

"Very well," said the policeman, giving Will another glance, "no, no one has reported seeing anyone hanging around the school. It's in a very quiet neighbourhood. If there had been anyone looking suspicious then I'm certain that someone would have seen them."

"Look, Max," Will said taking hold of his sister's hand, "now that Brian's back I think that Marie and I will go and see if we can find J."

"Sounds like you might know where to look," said the policeman suspiciously.

"Hang on just a minute pal," Brian said angrily looming over the policeman, "what's that meant to mean?"

"Easy now, sir," said the policeman, eager to calm the huge man down, "I'm just doing my job."

"Yes Well, why don't you go and do it outside," Brian said, his anger at the accusation aimed at Will only just held in check, "before I decide to do something that we both might regret.

Billings thought for a moment about arresting Brian for threatening him, but he knew that his comment had been wrong and that the big man was truly emotional. There was also the simple but undeniable fact that the man in front of him was built like a mountain and Billings had enough sense to not try and arrest someone like that without at least another two officers and perhaps a very large dog.

"I'd better go and radio in," Billings said trying his best to save face.

The four of them watched the young policeman walk out of the house. Once he was gone Brian said softly, "idiot."

"Do you have any idea where he might have gone, Will?" Max said turning to her brother hopefully.

"Not really, Max," Will answered, "but there's not much we can do here and it's better if he's found by us rather than some stranger."

"Alright," Max said letting go of his hand, "but please phone even if you don't find him at least I'll know what's going on."

"Of course we will," Will said as he and Marie started towards the door, "and Brian."

"Yes Will," Brian said looking round at his brother-in-law.

"Thanks for standing up for me then."

"No problem, BB," Brian said with a smile, "now go and find our little J and bring him home to us."

Will and Marie didn't say anything until they were streets away from Max's house.

"He's at the lodge, isn't he?" Marie asked, more a statement than a question.

"Yes, I think he is," Will said reluctantly, "where else could he be."

"What do we do?"

"We go and get him back," Will said, the edge in his voice sending a small shiver of fear down Marie's back and suddenly she was very glad that she was on Will's side and that he was not coming for her.

The pair of them drove as fast as they could through the centre of town without attracting attention. About five minutes from the lodge Marie's phone rang and despite the seriousness of the situation the force of habit was too much, and she answered her phone without thinking.

"Oh, hi, Carol," she said as she continued to look out of the passenger side window in the forlorn hope that she would see Jason walking along.

"No, I'm sorry babe," she said still looking out of the window, "but something's serious has come up so we're not going to be able to come."

"Alright then," Marie said after pausing for her friend to speak, "I'll call you when I can "

Once she'd had hung up and put her phone back into her bag Will said, "everything alright?"

"Yes," she said not taking her eyes from the view outside, "that was just my friend Carol, and she's got an eclipse party this afternoon. I was going to take you and J to it."

Suddenly Marie sat bolt upright in her seat and shouted, "oh my god, Will stop the car."

Will slammed his foot down so hard onto the brake pedal that the car went into a skip. Once it came to a stop the tyres were smoking like a dragster taking off from the starting line of a race.

"What is it?" Will said excitedly, "is it J, have you seen him?"

"No, Will not J," she said just as excitedly as Will, "the eclipse."

"What are you talking about?" Will said starting to get angry," I don't understand."

Marie took a deep breath as she tried to put her thoughts in order.

"Ok listen," she said slowly, "all this time we've thought that the only time that Otto could be destroyed was on the 21st of December, right?"

"Yes, that's right," Will said agreeing with her but still not really understanding what she was saying.

"But that's not the darkest of days," Marie said with a smile, "that's just the shortest day."

"But that's the same, isn't it?" Will asked still more than a little confused.

"That's what I thought until just a moment ago," Marie said excitedly," remember that strange little rhyme that Martha told us."

"Yes, I do," Will said with a shiver, "and it still creeps me out. How did it go? On the darkest of days with night in the afternoon if we find his soul and take it beyond the threshold of the lodge he will be destroyed."

"That's it the darkest of days, don't you get it, the darkest of days is not the shortest day. It's when the moon passes in front of the sun. It's the eclipse and it's going to happen today at three this afternoon."

Will sat there in his car stunned by what he'd just heard. All these years Martha and her children had been trying to find Otto's soul on the twenty-first of December and even if they had it would have done them no good whatsoever. How that must have appealed to Otto's cruel and evil nature. To give them such a glimmer of hope only to know that it would never work.

"Three," Will said as he looked at the clock on the dashboard in front of him, "that only gives us just over two hours."

"Then we'd best get moving, BB," she said grimly, "so put your foot down."

As they drove the rest of the way they talked about where Otto might have hidden his soul.

"I bet it's somewhere prominent," Will said as he weaved in and out of the traffic, "that would appeal to his nature. Put it somewhere obvious."

"But where?" Marie asked as she tried to imagine where such a thing could be hidden and in what, "I mean it's got to be something that's never moved, something that's so much part of the lodge that no one would ever think about taking it away or for that matter even touching it."

"I know where it is," Will said suddenly, "that tricky bastard. I know where he put it."

"But where?" Marie said still trying to think, "Where would it."

Marie stopped in mid-sentence as Will words came back to her.

"Somewhere prominent, somewhere obvious."

"Oh, Will I get it, it's the."

"Yes, that's right," Will said smiling coldly, "it's in that bloody great picture."

"The cheeky sod," Marie said unable to suppress a smile, "all this time it's been right under Martha's nose. I bet he must have loved that."

"I bet he did," Will said as they pulled into the lodge's car park, "but we're going to wipe that smile right off of his smug little face."

They both found it strange to pull into the lodge's car park in the middle of the day and find it completely deserted. Will didn't bother to park in one of the bays he just drove right up to the main doors and parked in front of them, as the pair of them got out a glint of sunlight caught Marie's eye.

"Will," she said taking hold of his arm, "look over there."

"What is it?" he asked squinting against the bright midday sun.

"It's Sally's car," Marie said coldly, "she must be here as well somewhere in the lodge."

Chapter Twenty-Six

As they walked through the large front doors of the now deserted lodge both Will and Marie could feel the emptiness of the place. The way the entrance hall echoed made the hairs stand up on both their necks.

"This is creepy," Marie said stepping closer to her boyfriend and taking hold of his arm.

"Are you scared little girl?" said a voice from just in front of them.

As they both looked in the direction of this new and quite unexpected voice, they saw a very changed Sally standing in front of them. Gone was the slightly frumpy looking head nurse and in her place stood the real Sally. Marie's former friend was now dressed in a tight pair of leather trousers, high heels and a tight-fitting bodice like top that extenuated her cleavage making it far bigger than it already was. The whole look should have made Sally look ridicules but instead, she looked incredible. It was as if a fire had been lit inside her and the heat from that fire was radiating out from her burning off the woman that was to reveal the real nature of the woman inside.

"Oh my god, Sally," Marie said when she saw how the other woman was dressed.

"Do you like it?" Sally asked smiling as she turned slowly around to show Marie the whole of her outfit.

"Where's J, you bitch," Will said unable to contain his anger any longer.

"Easy now boy," Sally said as she reached into the alcove beside her and dragged out a tied up and terrified Jason.

"Jason," Will shouted when he saw his nephew.

"Like I said, Will," Sally said as she drew a wicked-looking knife from her belt and held it under Jason's neck, "easy."

"How did you manage to get him out of the playschool?" Will asked as he looked into the frightened eyes of his young nephew.

"That was so easy," Sally said as she ran her hand almost lovingly through Jason's hair, "Otto had this stupid child eating out of his hands, it was a simple matter to get Jason here to hid in the school and then sneak through a window that I'd managed to open. He didn't even realise anything was wrong until I tied him up when we got here and then did, he scream."

"What's happened to you, Sally?" Marie asked as she watched Sally smile as the tears ran freely down Jason's face.

"I woke up," Sally said venomously, "I woke up and realised that I had nothing. No husband, no life, no future and that was when Otto offered me everything, immortality, power, excitement everything I ever wanted and so much more."

"And all you have to do is torture innocent children to get it, is that right?"

"No," Sally said her smile growing even wider, "not just that. You must enjoy it as well and I do, I truly do."

"You bitch," Marie said her voice filled with as much venom as Sally's had been, "if you didn't have hold of little J I'd kick the shit out of you."

"Why don't you try," said a deeper voice from behind Sally.

As Will and Marie watched Otto Crabtree the monster of Crabtree lodge materialised behind Sally.

"Would you like to fight her my dear?" Otto said as he ran his hand across Sally's face and down to her breast.

"Yes, I would," Sally said, as she pushed Jason into the waiting arms of Otto, "she's always been a moaning little cow. It'll be good to finally shut her up."

"Come on then you bitch," Marie said stepping forward.

"Are you mad, Marie, she'd crazy," Will said grabbing her by the arm.

Marie turned so that neither Sally nor Otto could see her face and mouthed the words. "Get the picture."

"Uncle Will," Jason said looking longingly at Will, "I'm scared."

"Now now," Otto said looking down at the young boy, "none of that. I think it's time you had a little nap, Jason."

Otto waved his hand in front of Jason's face in a complicated gesture and after only a few moments Jason yawned and slumped against the wall he only just managed to sit on the floor before he fell into a deep dreamless sleep

"Now that's we have no distractions," Otto said with a smile as he rubbed his hands together, "I can enjoy the entertainment."

As Marie stepped forward towards Sally Will couldn't help but step forward with her.

"Stay where you are," Otto said pointing at Will, "If you interfere, I'll take the boy now."

Will took a few steps backwards never taking his eyes from Otto for a moment. Otto returned his stare and said, "All in good time boy. You'll get your chance at me but for the moment just enjoy the fight."

Will didn't get a chance to reply as Sally screamed incoherently and rushed Marie slapping her hard across the face and sending her crashing into the corridor wall. Marie shook her head and wiped a small drop of blood from the corner of her lip.

"I would have thought you could hit harder than that, "Marie said with a smile, "what with all that weight you can put behind it."

Sally screamed again as she lashed out. But this time Marie was ready for her and caught Sally's hand before it could reach her face. She then stepped in close to her former friend and punched her as hard as she could in the face. Sally's nose exploded with blood, but she didn't fall. Instead, she grabbed a handful of Marie's hair and spun her around until the pair of them collapsed onto the floor biting and scratching at each other.

Will looked from the fight to where Otto was standing. The man who had built the lodge and now walked its halls as a ghost was completely captivated by the two women fighting. The smile that Will saw on his face was something that he hoped he would never have to see again, it was a smile full of evil born of the pain of others. The blood that Marie and Sally were shedding was exciting Otto like a shark coming in for the kill. Will took a step backwards stopped to see if it had been noticed then took another and another until he was standing at the junction of the corridors. He took one last look before he turned and dashed towards the picture that hung by the front doors of the lodge. As Will grabbed at the picture a voice from behind him said, "What are you doing?"

Will turned with the picture in his hands to see Otto standing in front of him.

"Get back," Will said holding the picture above his head, "take one step and this goes right out the window.

"Don't be hasty now, Will," Otto said holding up his hands, "let's talk about this."

"Martha," Will shouted still holding on to the painting, "help me."

"Those cowards won't help you, boy," Otto said confidence filling his voice, "so put the painting down and we'll talk."

"I don't think so," Will said as he edged towards the window, "as long as I've got this, you're not going to do anything to me. Now call your pit bull off Marie and let my nephew go."

"Sally," Otto shouted, "let her go."

A few moments later Sally and Marie walked over to where Will and Otto were standing. Both women were covered in blood, Marie had a huge black eye and Sally's face was coved in scratch marks from Marie's fingernails

"How are you doing?" Will asked Marie as she walked over to him.

"I've been better," she answered as she gingerly touched her lip that had already begun to swell, "what happens now?"

Before Will could answer Martha and Phillip stepped out of the shadows that lurked by the lodge's front doors.

"What's happening, Will," Martha asked looking from the young man with the picture held over his head to the monster of Crabtree lodge.

"We figured it out, Martha," Will said edging even closer to the window by the door, "the riddle, where Otto has hidden his soul, the whole thing."

"Really, Will," Martha said hope blossoming in her voice, "you have?"

"Night in the afternoon is the eclipse," Will said, "and he put his soul in the one thing that would never be moved, his picture."

"Are you sure, Will?" Phillip asked stepping towards the young man in front of him, "are you sure?"

"If I'm wrong Phillip then how come I'm still alive," Will said nodding towards Otto, "why haven't he killed both me and Marie or at the very least attacked us?"

"He right, Martha," Phillip said, happy for the first time in decades, "look at Otto he's scared. We've got him, Martha; we've got him at last."

"If you put the picture down boy," Otto said ignoring Martha and Phillip, "I will let you the girl and your nephew leave here, and I can tell you where to find more gold than you will need for the rest of your life."

"Gold," Will said his arms dropping just a little at the mention of treasure, "what do you mean gold."

"When I was alive, "Otto said, never taking his eyes from the picture, "I buried gold and jewels I stole from patients. You can have it all if you want. All you have to do is put the picture down and walk away."

Will looked from Otto into the sadly hopeful faces of the long-dead nurse and her young charge. Will would have been a liar to himself if he had said that Otto's offer had not for a moment tempted him but as he looked at Martha and Phillip, he knew that he would never be able to live with himself if he just walked away and left the poor souls of Crabtree lodge to the tender mercies of Sir Otto Crabtree. Will smiled at Martha and Phillip as he said, "you know what Otto, you're a scumbag."

Then as hard as he could Will threw the large ornate picture through the window and out into the lodge's car park.

Otto screamed as the painting went through the window and into the outside world. Will watched as Otto covered his face with his hands and sank to his knees screaming all the time.

"We're free, Martha," Phillip said a savage smile spreading across his face, "we're free at last.

"Otto no," Sally shouted as she knelt beside the creature that had offered her immortality in return for what was essentially her soul, "what about us what about all the things we'd planned. Please don't leave me alone."

Otto screamed again and fell from his knees into a ball onto the floor.

"Can this be true?" Martha said as she watched the tormentor of her adopted children writhing on the floor in agony, "are we free?"

"Look what you've done;" Sally shouted at Will, "you've taken him from me."

"Good," Will said without a hint of compassion in his voice, "now at least he's getting a taste of what those poor children have had to suffer all these years."

"Children," Martha said, at last, believing the evidence of her own eyes, "children come to me. We are free."

A few moments later the last children of the lodge stepped out of the shadows behind Martha and started at their tormentor as he lay on the floor screaming.

"Watch children," Martha said coldly as she stepped towards Otto, "watch this monster die."

As the children stepped towards Otto he screamed again. The group of children stepped back in fright then slowly edged forward once again. They stared in fascination as Otto lay on the floor his movement gradually becoming slower and weaker until suddenly, he stopped moving completely.

"Is he dead?" Phillip asked as he stared at Otto's unmoving body, "I mean is he dead like we can die?"

Just before Martha could answer a small snigger came from the prone body that lay beside Sally. This snigger grew into a chuckle that itself grew into a roaring belly laugh. Martha and the children stepped back in horror as Otto rose to his feet, his face red with laughter.

"That was the best fun I've had in a hundred years," he said as he put his arm around Sally and bowed towards Will and Marie, "thank you so much for the opportunity to show off my acting ability that's something I've not done since I was a boy."

"But the picture?" Will said unable to understand what had happened.

"The picture, boy," Otto said real humour in his voice, "do you think I would be that much of a fool as to put my soul inside something as fleeting as a picture that could be stolen or put to the flame. No boy you will have to do much better than that."

Martha's children screamed and ran back into the shadows only Martha and Phillip dared to stay and watch what happened. Otto, once he had finished talking to Will turned to the other two ghosts and said, "did you think you would be rid of me? I am going to be here for a long time, and you and I Phillip are going to have so much fun, even more than we have had so far."

Phillip his heart and hope broken by the fact that Otto did not die crumpled to the floor and softly began to cry.

"Music to my ears," Otto said as he listened to Phillip's sobs.

"You basted," Will said as he jumped at Otto.

Otto caught Will easily by the throat and then slapped him hard across the face.

"Did you think I could not touch you boy," Otto said as he watched blood start to flow out of Will's lip, "looks like that was something else you were wrong about doesn't it?"

"Let him go," Marie said stepping forward to help Will.

"Don't worry my sweet," Otto said smiling at Marie as Sally grabbed her former friend in a savage arm lock, "I'll get round to you soon enough."

"Martha, help him," Marie shouted as her arm was twisted hard up her back.

"Don't blame poor old Martha my sweet," Otto said enjoying himself immensely, "without my soul there is nothing that she can do to stop me."

Otto dragged Will to the opposite side of the front doors to the unbroken window.

"Now I think it's time you joined my poor old picture," Otto said as he picked Will up and with a heave threw him out into the car park.

Will landed heavily on the concrete in a shower of flying glass. The last thing that Will heard as unconsciousness started to wrap its warm embrace around him was Marie's scream and Otto's hearty evil laughter.

Chapter Twenty-Seven

"Now that's one problem dealt with," Otto said rubbing his hands together, "I think it's time to have some fun."

"What are we going to do, Otto? Sally asked pushing Marie's arm even further up her back.

Marie refused to scream but the pain from her arm forced tears from her eyes.

"The first of many my sweet I promise," Otto said pointing to Marie's tears as they ran down her cheeks, "I don't know if you'll join us here, but your screams will roam this place for a very long time."

"It's going to be fun to hurt you," Sally said almost lovingly in Marie's ear.

The pain in Marie's arm made it impossible for her to answer but she still refused to scream.

"You are a strong one, aren't you?" Otto said walking up to Marie and running his hand down her cheek, "I like that. It's no fun breaking someone without a spirit."

"Please don't hurt her, Otto," Martha said walking up and standing beside her long time enemy, "can't you just let this one go."

"Are you begging me, Martha?" Otto asked turning to look at Martha," you're not on your knees so you can't be begging."

Martha, her face red with a mixture of anger and embarrassment started to sink slowly to her knees.

"Don't bother," Otto off handily, "this one is going to be too much fun to even think about giving up."

Marie saw the look of sympathy and sorrow in Martha's eyes when Otto said this and that look more than anything else that afternoon made her blood turn to ice.

As Martha turned to walk over to console the still crying Phillip, Otto said, "he was right about one thing you know Martha, it is the eclipse. That's the key but once that's past this afternoon there is nothing that anyone can do to me for the next hundred and twenty-two years, and what fun those years will be."

"Why can't you just die, Otto?" Martha said as she sat down and put her arm around Phillip, "why can't you just die?"

"Now, Martha," Otto said happily, "is that any way to talk to a friend?"

"What are we going to do to her, Otto," Sally asked twisting Marie's arm even harder.

Despite her best efforts, this new burst of pain, at last, managed to squeeze a cry from between Marie's lips.

"It seems you can scream," Otto said with an evil smile, "let's see if we can make you scream again."

Out in the car park, Will drifted slowly back to consciousness. At first, he couldn't quite place where he was. It was Marie's scream brought him truly back to life.

"Marie," he said as he jumped up and ran towards the front doors of the lodge.

Will pulled on the door handle but no matter how hard he pulled, the doors would not move.

"Marie," he shouted banging his fists on the doors.

His only answer was another screamed forced from Marie by Sally's merciless grip on her arm. Will left the doors and ran to the now smashed windows. He jumped up onto the windowsill but no matter how hard he tried Will could not get through whatever unseen barrier Otto had placed there. All he could do was look into the lodge and watch helplessly as Sally hurt Marie repeatedly.

"Let her go you, bitch," Will shouted as he tried desperately to get through the window.

"There's nothing you can do boy," Otto said with a smile as he walked up to stand on the other side of the broken window, "I control this place. No one can enter here if I do not wish it. So why don't you go home, forget about your girlfriend and your little nephew and think yourself lucky that I'm more interested in them than I am in you."

"Let them go you bastard," Will said banging his fists on the barrier that barred his way, "let them go."

"You're boring me now," Otto said off handily, "go away."

Otto waved his hand at the widow and the barrier that was holding Will back suddenly pushed forward and threw him from the windowsill so that he landed hard, back on the concrete of the car park for the second time in ten minutes.

As Will lay there, despair placing its icy hand on his heart the moon began its slow journey across the face of the sun.

"It's started," Will said to the empty car park, "and there's nothing I can do."

"Can you hear me, boy," Otto shouted victory echoing in his voice, "the eclipse has started I can feel it and once it's finished the lodge, the children and your woman will all be mine."

Once again Will got to his feet; he couldn't think what to do. He couldn't get into the lodge, and he couldn't save Marie or J or the others. He knew he couldn't just walk away but he couldn't just stand there and listen to another scream from Marie either. Will looked about for something stronger than just his fists to hit the door with if he could just get inside then at the very least, he might be able to get Marie and Jason out. As the sky grew darker with the growing eclipse Will ran to the small gardening hut that sat just at the edge of the car park. The door was locked but that was no barrier to Will frustration. It only took two kicks at the aged lock before the door flew back on its hinges. Will went inside and after a quick search found a large sledgehammer. He ran back to the front door of the lodge to start his forlorn attempt at entry. The darkness was almost complete as Will swung the sledgehammer. But he misjudged his swing and the heavy sixteen pounds of metal struck the motto inscribed arch just above the doors.

Inside the lodge, Otto was halfway through unbuttoning Marie's top when suddenly he stopped he stepped back from her, gasped and all the colour ran from his face.

"Will," Marie shouted when she saw the look on Otto's face, "whatever you're doing do it again."

"Stop him," Otto gasped at Sally, "Stop him now."

Sally let go of Marie and ran as fast as she could for the lodge's car park.

In the car park Will heard Marie's shouted instruction but at first, didn't understand what she meant. Then he looked up at the arch above the doors and saw the hairline crack in it that his sledgehammer had caused. Then suddenly his first day at the lodge came flooding back into Will's mind. His first meeting with Marie and her translation of the lodge's motto, Animus Est Vita, the soul is all. Then just as suddenly Otto's words of only a few moments ago replaced Marie's.

"Would I put my soul in something as fleeting as a picture that could be stolen or put to the flame?"

"You put it in the building itself," Will said looking up at the arch, "and left a clue for everyone to see. The soul is all."

Before Will could swing the sledgehammer again the lodge's doors were swung open and Sally, screaming like a banshee came rushing towards him. If Will had had more than a moment to think then maybe he would have not reacted the way he did. But he had no time at all to think as Sally rushed at him. Will took one step backwards and as Sally reached him he jabbed at her with the sledgehammer striking her squarely in the forehead with the flat head of the hammer. Sally was sent flying back through the lodge's front door coming to rest unconsciously at Marie's feet.

"Bitch," Marie said as she drew her foot back and kicked Sally squarely in the ribs.

Otto, now totally ignoring Marie ran to the front door and shouted to Will, "Stop, I can give you anything you want, just stop."

Will looked at Otto and for the first time saw him for what he truly was, a cowardly bully only interested in hurting anyone weaker than himself.

Will didn't answer he just swung the sledgehammer again this time striking the arch full on. The old stone split but didn't break. Otto screamed as the hammer struck and this time his scream was real, a scream full of pain and fear. Otto fell to his knees and said, "I'm begging you stop, please stop."

"How many poor souls have said that to you, Otto?" Will said as he started to swing the hammer again, "did you ever listen to them?"

Will's third and last swing smashed the arch asunder sending shards of stone flying everywhere.

"I see it, Otto," Martha screamed in triumph, "I see your soul."

As the moon closed over the sun completely and night came to the afternoon a small bronze container fell from the arch and rolled through the doors of the lodge stopping just at Martha's feet, the protector of the children of Crabtree lodge bend down and tentatively picked it up.

"Please, Martha," Otto said crawling towards the nurse on his knees, "don't."

Martha looked down at the tormenter of her adopted children and without a word, she broke open the cylinder and threw it as hard as she could beyond the threshold of the lodge. As the bronze cylinder hit the car park Otto screamed a final time and then he started to shrink and fade. The pain that etched itself on Otto's face made Marie look away. But the children who he had tortured for so long gathered around him and watched his final agonising moments in silence. Otto continued to shrink, folding in on himself becoming smaller until only his screams could be heard but they, in turn, faded away until nothing was left of Otto Crabtree but a bad dream.

"What happened?" Sally said groggily getting to her feet, "where's Otto?"

"He's gone, Sally," Marie said icily, "we killed him."

"No," Sally said sinking to her knees, "he can't be gone."

"But he is," Phillip said walking up to the kneeling Sally, "and now you're left here with us."

Sally, her eyes filled with fear knelt motionless as the children of the lodge gathered around her.

"Marie, please help me," she shouted stretching out her hands to her former friend.

"I'm sorry, Sally," Marie said turning her back on Sally, "there's nothing I can do."

Phillip and the other children took hold of Sally and dragged her into the shadows disappearing with her in an instant.

"Where have they taken her, Martha?" Marie asked unsure if she wanted to know the answer or not.

"They've taken her to the in-between," Martha said a little sorrow in her voice.

"The in-between?" Marie asked, "What's that?"

"Trust me," Will said stepping up beside her and putting his arm around her waist, "you don't want to know."

Before Marie could ask what he meant, Phillip and the other children stepped out of the shadows without Sally.

Will felt a small shiver run down his spine and despite himself, he could not help but feel sorry for Sally, lost and alone in the terrible in-between for eternity. For a moment Will wondered to himself if anyone truly deserved that kind of punishment. Then he thought about what she and Otto had planned for Jason and any compassion that he had felt for her vanished.

"Can we leave now Martha?" Phillip asked his voice sounding old and weary.

"Yes, dear," Martha said with a smile, "we can, we all can."

"Goodbye, Martha," Will said as he watched the children gather around the nurse.

"Thank you, Will," Martha said smiling at him, "if it wasn't for you, we would never have been free."

"Goodbye," Marie said as she watched the children and Martha begin to fade.

Just before they all vanished Margery ran from the group and swung her arms around Will's neck kissing him lightly on the cheek.

"Thank you," she said sweetly, and then she ran back and grabbed hold of Phillip's outstretched hand

Marie and Will stood and watched as the small group of ghosts became increasingly insubstantial until they were nothing more than a memory and the lodge was just an empty old building.

"Uncle Will," Jason said waking up from Otto's spell.

"Hello, J," Will said happily, walking over to his nephew and picking him up.

"I want to go home, Uncle Will," Jason said as he put his arms around his uncle's neck.

"You know what, J," Will said as he carried Jason over to Marie, "so do I."

Will took hold of his girlfriend's hand and the three of them walked out of the lodge and into the sunlight of a beautiful afternoon.

The End

Did you love *Animus Est Vista*? Then you should read *Requiem of Shadows*[1] by Drue Fairlie!

Kate Wright, a young police officer is set to investigate the disappearance of three young men on a night out. Her investigation leads her to police corruption and, what she first believes to be human trafficking. But things are not always what they first appear to be. And soon Kate is involved in matters darker than she could ever have imagined.180,000 people go missing in the united kingdom each year.Where do they go?To Old Town they do go.

---

1. https://books2read.com/u/baB5wx

2. https://books2read.com/u/baB5wx

About the Author

Drue Fairlie is a writer, and author of many books such as "The Catspaw Incident and Old Town" He has spent most of his years researching and writing fiction novels about extraordinary characters and the intoxicating adventures they ensue. Drue has been a collaborative writer in the works of other authors and enjoys travelling where he finds the inspiration for his stories and characters. Drue lives currently in Madisonville Kentucky USA. He was married in December 2019 to Candace Michelle Fairlie. He enjoys watching wrestling, vintage Hammer films, and Isle of Jura whiskey. He has a knack for historical facts and trivia. His family is his world.